JAMES HADLEY CHASE

'Chase is one of the very rare thriller writers capable of always replying intelligently to the question: "What happens next?" He must be considered as one of the greatest story tellers of today, if his inventiveness, his feeling for a situation and absolute personal style are taken into consideration.'
– *La Revue de Paris*

'He has such a strong, intelligent, highly-tuned thriller-talent that he goes drifting past opposition like Jim Clark through a school of commuter cowboys. He takes off smoothly on a theme and is doing the ton before you notice. You may be horrified by his characters, but your sympathy races along with them. He makes no pit-stops, like other writers, but goes on driving at the point of issue; and though you may be sometimes hanging on to your stomach you never ask him to let you get out.'
– *Eastern Daily Press*

'He can write all but a very few of his competitors into the ground.'
– *Time and Tide*

James Hadley Chase

An Ace Up My Sleeve

CORGI BOOKS

AN ACE UP MY SLEEVE
A CORGI BOOK 0 552 09424 2

Originally published in Great Britain by
Robert Hale and Co.

PRINTING HISTORY
Robert Hale edition published 1971
Robert Hale edition reprinted 1971
Corgi edition published 1973
Corgi edition reprinted 1977
Corgi edition reissued 1980
Corgi edition reissued 1986

This book is set in 10 on 10½ pt Baskerville

Corgi Books are published by Transworld Publishers
Ltd., 61–63 Uxbridge Road, Ealing, London W5 5SA, in
Australia by Transworld Publishers (Aust.) Pty. Ltd.,
26 Harley Crescent, Condell Park, NSW 2200, and in New
Zealand by Transworld Publishers (N.Z.) Ltd., Cnr. Moselle
and Waipareira Avenues, Henderson, Auckland.

Set, printed and bound in Great Britain by
Cox & Wyman Ltd., Reading, Berks.

This one is for my four Aces:

Sylvia
Bru
Tracey Lee
and
Hervey

CHAPTER ONE

HELGA ROLFE crossed the lobby of the Königshof Hotel, her mink coat draped over her shoulders, aware that two stout German business men were eyeing her, their eyes taking in the coat, the black two piece suit, the red blouse and the mink trimmed hat. The eyes approved, but by now, she was used to approving male eyes. Approval no longer interested her: she needed more than approval.

She dropped her room key on the desk and the Hall Porter, bowing, gathered it up as if it were a thing of value.

'You need your car, madame?'

His guttural English irritated her. She spoke German, French and Italian fluently, but he knew her to be an American and to him, all Americans spoke only English.

'No . . . I'm shopping.' She spoke in German. 'I am leaving tomorrow at eight o'clock. Please have my car serviced and ready.'

The Hall Porter's fat fingers closed on a pencil and he made a note.

'Yes, madame.' He persisted in his English. 'Then at eight. I will have your account ready. Is there anything else?'

She shook her head as she slid her arms into the coat before a page could move to help her. Giving the disappointed boy a smile, she left the hotel.

The sky above Bonn was the colour of lead, and it was cold. Already flakes of snow were falling to disappear on the sidewalk, making it wet and slippery.

Helga hated the cold. Her body cringed inside the comfort of her expensive coat and she walked briskly, trying to stir her blood, pampered by the excessive heating of the hotel.

She walked under the arch of the University, paused to let a stream of fast moving cars go by, then crossing the street,

7

she headed towards the shopping centre where cars are for-bidden.

The time was 11.35. She had slept late. She had gone to her room the previous evening immediately after dinner. What could a woman do on her own in any big city after dinner except go to bed? She knew the Maître d'hotel re-garded her as a nuisance when she came into the restaurant on her own, but he was impressed by her mink stole and her diamonds. He gave her service because he knew he would be well tipped. She had eaten quickly, enduring the steady stares from the fat German business men, eating alone and wondering about her. As soon as the meal was finished, she had left and taken the elevator to her room. The sleeping pills were on the bedside table. Sleep was her antidote to loneliness.

Now, walking briskly, she plunged into the crowds moving along the traffic empty streets, aware that women were eyeing her coat with envy. It was a beautiful coat, chosen by her husband when he had had one of his infrequent moods to please her. She knew that mink was now old hat, but to her, it was still luxury and still elegant. At her age, what did it matter? Her age? She paused to look in a mirror at the back of a shop window. Forty? Or was it forty-three? Why bother about three years? She studied her slim figure, the carefully made-up face with its high cheek bones, its large violet coloured eyes, the short, rather beautiful nose. Forty-three? She looked thirty, even with the east wind like an icy shroud around her.

Her eyes shifted from her own reflection to the reflection of a tall man standing across the way, apparently looking at her. The peaked baseball cap, the black leather jerkin, the faded blue jeans and the red cowboy shirt told her as nothing else could he was a compatriot. He was young – probably under twenty years and he was chewing gum. Bonn was full of Americans: soldiers on furlough, young people thumbing a ride through Europe and the inevitable tourists. Helga had lived long enough in Europe to despise most Americans abroad. This gum-chewing habit revolted her. She turned and walked into one of the big stores. She wanted tights, but she paused before a counter displaying woollen pants and

8

she looked enviously at them. Her body was cold, but she resisted the appeal of promised warmth in this Victorian garment. Suppose she had an accident? It would be shaming to be undressed, even by a nurse, to reveal she was swarthed in wool.

Having made her purchase, she loitered in the warmth of the store, idly looking at the merchandise, then aware time was moving, she braced herself and walked out into the east wind.

The gum-chewing. American was lolling against a lamp post, his hands thrust into the pockets of his jeans. She looked more closely at him, and she felt a sudden sexual desire stab through her. He was quite magnificent, she thought. There was a virility like a plasma coming from him. He had Slav features: a square-shaped face; large, widely spaced eyes and a short, blunt nose. He had immediate boyish charm.

She shifted her eyes and walked on. What was she thinking of? she asked herself. He was young enough to be her son, and she was angry with herself to feel so sexually moved.

She turned down another shopping street, making an effort not to look around to see if he were following her. Why should he? A kid ... young enough to be her son. She paused to look at a display of shoes. The display had no interest as her shoes were hand made, but it gave her the excuse to examine the mirror at the back of the window. She was in time to see he had followed her and was waiting, his broad shoulders finding another lamp post.

Her hands turned into fists as she felt a surge of hot blood go down to her loins. She was now unaware of the wind and the cold and, as if in flight, she began to walk away from him. Could he be interested in her? she asked herself. She passed a young, blonde girl, wearing stretch pants, so tight across her buttocks, she could have been naked. She had the knowing face of a woman who knows everything and yet is young enough still to remain enthusiastic. Helga looked enviously at her, thinking: 'When he sees this little tart, he'll forget to follow me.'

She entered a coffee shop and sat down, away from the

window. As she stripped off her gloves and took off her coat, the waitress came over and Helga asked for a coffee. She would not allow herself to look out of the window. With unsteady fingers, she lit a cigarette. She spent a disciplined half hour over her coffee, determined to be sure. If he was still waiting, then she would speak to him. She suddenly found herself muttering a prayer that he would be waiting.

At exactly 12.30, she crushed out her cigarette, paid her check, put on her coat and walked out into the street.

He was standing across the way, still chewing gum, still with his hands thrust into his jeans' pockets. She made to approach him, then stopped. Although she was now convinced he wanted to contact her, she was suddenly frightened of the possible result.

She turned abruptly and began walking towards her hotel. She had gone only a few yards when she stopped and turned. He was just behind her. They looked at each other and he touched the peak of his cap, a boyish, embarrassed grin lighting up his face.

'What do you want?' she asked.

People moved impatiently around them. They were like two rocks in a rushing stream.

Now close to him, she could feel his animal, youthful magnetism so strongly it made her feel weak.

His smile widened.

'Well, ma'am, you look kind of friendly,' he said. His voice was soft and he spoke carefully, making each word distinct. 'You're the first kind looking American I've seen since hitting this town. Excuse me. If I'm bothering you, just say so and I'll scram.'

'No ... you're not bothering me.' She was furious with herself that her voice sounded so emotional.

A fat man, wearing a leather hat with a feather in it brushed against her, making her give ground. A girl in a mini skirt, her fat legs purple with the cold, stepped around her while looking at this big boy who chewed on his gum. Helga felt a thrill of pride that he didn't even look at this girl as she tossed her unwashed hair in passing him.

There was a pause, then Helga said, 'I'm going to have lunch. Are you hungry?'

His grin widened.

'I sure am, ma'am. The fact is I'm broke and haven't eaten for two days.'

She felt suddenly depressed. Clever boy! she thought. So you've found a lonely woman, old enough to be your mother, and you're putting on the bite.

'Two's company ... I don't like eating alone,' she said. 'Eat with me.'

She turned and walked along the street until she came to the first cheap restaurant. He walked behind her and she could hear him humming. Why not? He was going to get a free meal.

She pushed open the glass door of the restaurant and then paused. She had never been in this class of restaurant before. If she were going to feed him, he had to be fed here. She couldn't take him back to the hotel. She couldn't face the Maître d'hotel if she took this boy into the luxury restaurant.

She looked around. Already, people were eating, and she saw with dismay, there were no tables for two. All the tables were set for six and all of them had people.

The boy seemed to know his way around. He touched her elbow and steered her to a table where two elderly Germans and their lumpy daughter were working through plates of boiled sausage and sauerkraut.

They stared up at Helga as she shed her coat. The boy took it from her and carefully hung it on a peg by the table. They sat down opposite each other. She found she was sitting too close to the German husband and she could feel his body heat. The boy opposite was sitting next to the daughter who squirmed away from him, then darted a smirking look at him. He didn't notice, his eyes searching for a waiter. The tightness of his face told Helga how hungry he was and she felt a pang of pity.

A waiter came, dropped two menus on the table, then went away to serve an order.

The boy looked at the handwritten menu and grimaced.

'Do you dig this, ma'am?' he asked anxiously. 'This language throws me.'

The waiter returned and looked first at Helga, then at the

boy as if trying to make up his mind who should have his attention, then the tilt of Helga's head told him she was going to order.

'Bean soup, steak and chips for one and an omelette for myself,' she said in German. 'Two beers.'

The waiter nodded and went away.

The three Germans at the table, hearing Helga's fluent German, looked curiously at her, then shifted their eyes.

'You speak the lingo, ma'am?' There was an admiring note in the boy's voice. 'That sure saves a lot of headaches.' He leaned forward, resting his big hands on the table. 'I'm Larry Stevens.'

She smiled.

'Helga Rolfe.'

'I'm from Nebraska.'

'Florida.'

There was a pause while he looked at her, his eyes admiring and she looked searchingly at him, her eyes hopeful.

'Wouldn't you be more comfortable if you took off your cap?' Immediately she said it, she regretted it. Americans seemed to live in their hats.

He flushed, then tore the cap off, shoving it out of sight under his thigh.

'Excuse me, ma'am. I guess I'm a hick. I forgot I'm wearing the goddamn thing.'

She looked at his close cut, blond hair and then studied his face. Again she felt hot blood move through her.

The beers arrived.

'You, me and the flag,' Larry said, picking up his glass and saluting her. He drank thirstily. Setting down his half empty glass with a sigh of content, he went on, 'I'm sure grateful.' He grinned at her: a warm, friendly grin that made her feel good. 'I thought I was really fixed.'

The food arrived. While she toyed with her omelette, she watched him eat. The three Germans at the table also watched. The soup disappeared. The big steak and the pile of potato chips went the same way. He ate with the concentration and the dedication of the starved. Every now and then, his mouth full, he looked up and grinned at her. The warmth of that grin was the nicest thing that had happened to her for a long time and she felt tears clouding her eyes. She frowned down at the remains of the omelette, not wanting him to see how moved she was.

The three Germans called for their bill and left the table. Larry laid down his fork.

'That was something, ma'am! That really was something!'

She saw the wistful look in his eyes as he regarded the empty plate and she signalled to the waiter.

'It was a success,' she said as he came quickly to her side. 'Please bring the order again.'

The waiter looked at Larry, then at her and he nodded, a big smile lighting up his fat face. He whipped away the plate and hurried towards the kitchen.

'What was that you said to him, ma'am?' Larry asked, peering at her.

'They always give double portions here,' Helga said. 'There's another steak coming.'

His grin was even more boyish.

'I appreciate it.' He leaned forward, looking directly at her. 'I want you to know, ma'am, I really appreciate this.' He shook his blond head. 'It's a funny thing, but when things look really tough, you get a sudden break. Ron told me that and I found it hard to believe. People do help out. You've helped me.' He sat back. 'Could be . . . I could help you and I'd be glad to.'

'You never know.' Her mind went quickly back into the past. There had been other people she had helped but they were now dim shadows. Because of her husband's position and his wealth no one had ever thought she might need help.

The steak and another pile of chips arrived.

'Excuse me, ma'am . . . this sure looks good.'

She lit a cigarette, her mind still in the past. Help? What is meant by help? she thought. It was easy to give money if you have money. No, that wasn't help . . . anyway, not to her. To share something . . . to blot out this awful loneliness . . . that was the kind of help she wanted and yet how few could or would give her that?

She came out of the past to watch him finish the steak. He laid down his fork and sat back.

'The best meal in years! I appreciate it, ma'am!'

The waiter came over and she ordered an apfel strudel with cream and coffees, then when he took the empty plate away, she said, 'What are you doing in Bonn?'

'That's a good question.' Larry laughed. 'I wish I knew. I guess I'm just passing through.' He leaned forward, his big hands clasped, his heavy shoulders hunched. 'I'm being educated. My old man told me to come to Europe and take a look around. He wanted me to see Europe before I settled down. So I've been getting around. I started in Copenhagen, came to Hamburg and now I'm here. My old man gave me some money, but I've lost it, so now I guess I'll have to find a job.' He shrugged, still smiling. 'I'll find something ... I haven't really looked yet. My old man doesn't want me back for another six months. He reckoned I'd run out of money. He told me it would be good for me if I did, so I could make a living while in Europe. My old man is very keen I should look after myself.' He paused, smiling at Helga. 'He's a real square, but I'm fond of him.'

The apfel strudel arrived and again there was silence while Larry ate. Then while they were sipping their coffees, she said, 'What do you plan to do?'

He lifted his shoulders.

'I'll look around. Someone must want something done, ma'am.'

'But you can't even speak the language.'

He laughed and she envied his confidence.

'I can always make myself understood.' He waved his hands. 'When you have hands, you don't need a language.'

She glanced at her watch. She had an appointment with her husband's attorney in half an hour.

'Do you want to come to Switzerland?' she asked, aware her heart was beating uncomfortably fast.

'Switzerland?' He looked questioningly at her. 'I don't mind where I go.'

'Can you drive a car?'

'Oh, sure.'

She opened her lizard skin handbag and took from it three one hundred DM bills.

'I am staying at the Königshof hotel. I am leaving for

14

Switzerland tomorrow morning at eight o'clock. I could use a spare driver. Do you want to come?'

Without hesitation he nodded.

'I sure would, ma'am.'

She slid the folded bills under her coffee saucer, then stood up and reached for her coat.

'Then I'll expect you.' She struggled into the coat while he sat there, looking up at her, his expression bewildered. 'Settle the check.' She smiled, aware her smile was too anxious. 'Goodbye for now, Larry.'

As he struggled to his feet, nearly overturning the table, she left the restaurant and walked out into the now heavily falling snow. For the first time in months, she felt young again.

She came out of a pill-induced sleep with a start of alarm, sure she had overslept. Turning on the bedside lamp, she looked anxiously at her travelling clock to find it was 06.50. She relaxed back on her pillow. Before going to bed she had packed two suitcases and had them taken down to the car. She now would have time to dress leisurely, she thought, and time to linger over a cup of coffee before leaving at 08.00.

She had gone over in her mind during the evening, while she had been eating her lonely dinner and while waiting for the pills to send her to sleep, this meeting with Larry Stevens.

When she thought of what she had done, she experienced a feeling of shame. She had acted like so many middle aged American women when they were abroad. Those awful women, trying to find late romance, who bore barmen, ogle hall porters and look feverishly for a lone man who would fill in the lonely hours before a car or a coach took them on yet another deadly sight-seeing tour.

But why be ashamed? she had reasoned with herself. Of course she had been stupid, but she had done nothing to make herself feel ashamed.

In fact, she told herself without much conviction, she had done a kindly act by feeding this boy and giving him money. With what she had given him, he could continue his journey until the money ran out and until he met yet another kind, lonely, stupid American woman . . . he wouldn't have far to look, she thought bitterly.

I could use a spare driver. Do you want to come?

That had been a mistake, but she didn't have to worry, she assured herself. He had her money . . . why should he want to come to Switzerland with a woman old enough to be his mother?

She began to think of him as he had sat opposite her in that squalid restaurant, eating, looking up at her from time to time, and of his warm, friendly grin. She wondered what it would be like to have him in this bed with her, and her body grew hot, moist and yielding at the thought. Angry with herself, she got out of bed and walked to the window. Pulling back the drapes, she looked down at the Rhine. The ferry steamer, packed with workers, was crossing from the far bank, its lights reflecting; in the leaden, cold looking river. Snow was falling, and had capped the church spires and the roofs of the distant factories.

It would be a dreary drive, she thought, along the monotonous autobahn to Basle. Then she would have to face the traffic of Zurich, the climb to the Bernadino tunnel and the long, difficult descent to Bellinzona. She grimaced and went to the bathroom.

Forty minutes later, the waiter brought her a pot of coffee. She was now dressed. Her mink coat lay across the chair, ready to put on. As the waiter entered, carrying the tray, she was adjusting her hat in the mirror, her eyes examining her make-up.

At three minutes to 08.00, she stubbed out her cigarette, put on her coat, gave herself one more quick glance in the mirror, then taking her handbag, she left the room.

She looked quickly around the lobby as she left the elevator. There was just a chance this tall, exciting boy might be there, waiting for her, but only a group of German business men and three pages met her eyes.

She paid her account and crossed to the Hall Porter to tip him.

'You should drive carefully, madame,' he said, palming the tip and becoming suddenly fatherly. 'The roads will be dangerous.'

16

She was in no mood for advice and she turned away to where the luggage porter was waiting.

'The luggage is in the boot, madame,' he said. His English was even worse than the Hall Porter's. 'The tank is full. The car is fully serviced.'

She tipped him and went out into the cold to the black Mercedes she had bought in Hamburg.

The porter and two pages went with her like bodyguards. She paused to look down the drive of the hotel. Snow was falling steadily: there was mist. She could see people hurrying along the sidewalk and beyond them the early morning traffic, but there was no sign of Larry Stevens.

She slid under the driving wheel. The porter closed the door with an elaborate bow and she shifted the gear lever to *Drive*. As the car began to move she glanced at her diamond studded wristwatch. The time was now 08.10.

The porter had run the car engine for some minutes so now the heater was operating. She turned on the wipers and edged the car down the drive feeling alone in spite of the security and luxury of the car, and feeling uneasy about facing the nine hundred kilometres of difficult road ahead of her.

She had guessed right, she thought bitterly. The boy had only wanted a free meal and her money. By now he was once more on his way, thinking she was just one more middle-aged sucker . . . which, of course, she was.

She had to stop at the junction as a stream of cars, edged by. Then she heard a soft tapping sound on the car window and she quickly turned her head, her heart-beat racing.

He was there, snow piled on the peak of his baseball cap, his face blue with the cold, his wide, friendly smile warming her. Suddenly she was years younger and suddenly stupidly happy. She waved to him to go around the car to the passenger's seat. He nodded, ran in front of the dipped headlights, paused to shake the snow from his cap, his leather jacket and his shoes. Then he opened the off side door, letting in a blast of cold air, and slid in beside her.

'Morning, ma'am.' His voice sounded as happy as she felt. 'Makes you think of Christmas, doesn't it?'

Yes, she thought. Christmas! He is really my Christmas present!

'Have you been waiting long? Why didn't you come to the hotel? You must be frozen.' She was pleased her voice was controlled.

'Not long, ma'am. I didn't think I should go to the hotel. That kind of hotel is snooty.' He laughed. 'This is a fine car ... is it yours?'

'Yes.' She slowed and stopped as the traffic lights turned to red. 'Where is your luggage, Larry?'

'I lost that with my money.'

'You mean you've nothing except what you've got on?'

He laughed.

'That's it. I sure walked into that one. Ron warned me. He said it could happen but I didn't believe him. There was this girl ... I thought she was okay, but I got rolled,' and he laughed again.

'You mean she stole your things?'

'Her boy friend did.' He shrugged. 'Ron warned me but I still fell for the act.' He grinned at her. 'Oh, ma'am before I forget: did you know you left three hundred marks to pay for that meal? I've got the change right here.' He took from his hip pocket a roll of bills.

'I meant you to keep that.'

'Oh, no!' His voice sharpened, and glancing at him, she saw he looked genuinely shocked. 'I accept free rides, but I don't accept money from anyone.'

She thought quickly.

'Then will you please keep it and pay for the gas when we need it?'

He looked at her from under the peak of his cap.

'Yeah ... sure.'

They were now approaching the entrance to the autobahn. The car's headlights showed her the road was flecked with snow and she thought there was a chance of black ice. As she joined the stream of traffic, she saw cars were moving with caution.

'We could be late getting to Basle,' she said.

'Are you in a hurry, ma'am?'

'No.'

18

'Nor me . . . I'm never in a hurry,' and he laughed.

No, she was now no longer in a hurry having him by her side. She had planned to get to the Adlon hotel in Basle by 14.00, but now she didn't care. Thinking about it, she realized it could be embarrassing to take Larry – with no luggage – to the Adlon. It would be better to find a much more modest hotel where there would be no questioning eyebrows.

'Where did you sleep last night?' she asked.

'I found a room. You'll excuse me, ma'am, but I had to use some of your money. I'll let you have it back.'

Another girl? She felt a stab of jealousy.

'Don't worry about that. I have plenty of money.' She hesitated, then went on, 'Money is useful, but it doesn't always bring happiness.'

He shifted, pushing up the peak of his cap, then pulling it down.

'My old man was always saying things like that.' She realized at once that she had said the wrong thing. 'People with plenty of money are always griping about happiness.' His voice had become surly.

'Yes . . . that's right.' She was anxious to go along with his views. 'When you have it, you don't always appreciate it.'

Again he shifted.

'People say that. Ron says too few people have too much money and too many have too little.'

Was that supposed to be wisdom? she thought, but she said, 'You keep mentioning Ron . . . tell me about him.'

'He's my buddy.' He turned to look at her and she was dismayed to see the elated expression on his face. Once, out of sheer boredom, she had gone to a Billy Graham meeting and she had been surrounded by simple people looking just the way this boy was looking now.

Again she felt a stab of jealousy, knowing he would never look like this if ever he talked about her to his friends.

'Tell me about him.'

He stared through the windshield for a long moment, then he said, 'I guess he's special. He's the smartest cookie I've ever known.' He shook his head in wonderment. 'You ask him anything . . . anything . . . and he comes up with the answer. You have a problem and he fixes it. He's really smart.'

'He sounds wonderful.' She was careful to make her voice sound enthusiastic. 'Where did you meet him?'

'Oh, I ran into him.' The way his voice dropped warned her this was none of her business.

'Why isn't he travelling with you?'

He laughed, slapping his big hand on his thigh.

'Right now, ma'am, he's in jail.'

'In jail!' Her voice shot up a note. 'But why?'

He looked at her, peering at her from under the peak of his cap.

'Don't think he's done anything wrong, ma'am. Sure, I know when you hear a guy is in jail you think he must be bad, but Ron's not like that. He's a protester. He staged this protest march in Hamburg so they put him in jail.'

With her hands resting lightly on the driving wheel, her eyes on the road ahead, Helga asked, 'What was he protesting about?'

There was a long pause and she glanced at him.

'What was he protesting about?' she repeated.

'I'm not too sure, ma'am.' He pulled at the peak of his cap. 'There was an awful lot of talk. All I know is he had good reason to protest.'

'What makes you think that?'

He shifted uneasily.

'He told me so.'

What a baby! she thought and she warmed to him.

'If he's as smart as you say he is, Larry, why is he in jail?'

'He is smart!' He nodded emphatically. 'He explained that to me. He told me if people don't know about you, you're nothing. He said publicity was the big thing. By getting tossed into jail, he got his photo in the papers. Right now, people are talking about him in Hamburg ... that's smart!'

'He is anti-rich, of course?'

Larry frowned.

'Yeah ... you could say that.'

'Are you anti-rich?'

'Maybe. I haven't thought about it much.'

'But you listen to Ron?'

'Sure ... you can't help listening to him! This Hamburg shindig was a ball! He got a bunch of guys together. I was one of them. It was raining fit to drown a duck. I wanted to stay under cover, but Ron wanted me out in front, so that's where I was.

'We were all standing there like corpses ... wet, hungry and cold. Then Ron started shooting the breeze. In five minutes he had us exploding like fire crackers. Man! That was something! We had a ball. We yelled, smashed shop windows, turned cars over and set fire to them. We threw bricks at the cops ... we had a real ball!'

'But why, Larry?'

He looked at her, his eyes suddenly hostile.

'It had to be done ... Ron said so.'

'Then what happened?'

'Well the cops got tough. They used these water cannons and Man! was it cold!' He laughed. She was relieved that his hostility had been just a brief passing thing. 'Then they used tear gas. It really got tough. Ron reached me. We were ankle deep in broken glass and there were five cars exploding ... it was like a battlefield. Everyone was yelling and fighting. He said for me to get out of Hamburg fast ... so I got out.'

It was now light enough to turn off the headlights and the snow had stopped. She increased the speed of the car.

'How long will he be in jail?' she asked.

'I don't know ... maybe a week.'

'Do you plan to see him again?'

'Sure, I'll see him again. I have his address. You don't find a guy like Ron and then lose him. I'll send him a card.' He nodded to himself as if a postcard solved all problems. 'I sure hope to see him again ... he's something special.'

His vagueness, Helga thought, could mean he wouldn't see this man again, and she felt relieved.

'You worry me,' she said. 'You have no luggage, no clothes, no money. I can't see how you are going to exist.'

'You don't have to worry about me, ma'am. I'll get by. I'll find a job.' He smiled confidently at her. 'It's nice of you to worry. I'll get a job in a hotel or a garage. I don't need much money.'

Ahead of her she saw a parking sign and she slowed the car.

'Would you like to drive?'

'I'd be glad to.'

She drove into the parking bay and stopped the car. He got out, walked around to the on side door as she slid over to the passenger's seat.

By the way he drove on to the autobahn, she knew immediately he was an expert driver. He had the car moving at 170 k.p.h. in a few minutes, and she felt not only slightly ashamed, but also elderly that she had been driving so cautiously.

'We'll be in Basle in a couple of hours at this rate,' she said.

'Am I driving too fast, ma'am?'

He was driving too fast, but she couldn't bring herself to admit it.

'No ... I like it. You drive very well.'

'Thank you, ma'am.'

By the slight frown on his face, she realized he didn't want to talk. He wanted to concentrate on his driving, enjoying the power of the car and showing her his expertise. She relaxed, and after watching the monotonous road racing towards her for some time, her mind drifted back into her past: something she caught herself doing as she grew older.

The only child of a brilliant international lawyer, Helga had received a continental education. She had had training in law and top class secretarial work. Her father had joined a firm in Lausanne, Switzerland, which specialized in tax problems. When she was twenty-four and fully qualified, he brought her into the firm as his personal assistant. She quickly made herself indispensable. The heart attack that killed her father some years later made no difference to her position with the firm. Jack Archer, one of the junior partners, grabbed her for his personal secretary before any of the senior partners thought of doing so. She knew she could have had her choice, but Archer appealed to her: he was handsome, dynamic and magnificently sexy. She had always been over-sexed. Men were necessary in her life, and she had had so many lovers she had lost count of their faces. When Archer had asked her to work with him and when she had nodded, he had locked his office door and by way of celebration they had had what she called a 'quickie' on the floor and which had proved satisfactory to both of them.

Somehow Jack Archer had got hold of Herman Rolfe's Swiss account. No one knew quite how he had done it: even he, himself, was unsure. Herman Rolfe had come to Lausanne in search of a top class lawyer and income tax consultant and somehow Archer had got himself noticed and got the job. This was a killing that promoted Archer to senior partner. The Rolfe account was as important to the firm as the White House is to a future President.

Herman Rolfe, tall, lean, balding, the wrong side of sixty-five, tough and ruthless, had built an empire around electronics that had made him one of the richest men in the world. Long ago he had seen the red light of pending currency restrictions and had, at first legally, then illegally, siphoned off the bulk of his money to a numbered account in Switzerland. He needed a good man on the spot to handle his instructions and chose Jack Archer. As Helga was Archer's personal assistant, she too became involved.

Every three months, Rolf flew into Geneva where Archer met him to discuss investments. On one pending visit, Archer broke a leg while ski-ing and asked Helga to take his place.

'You have all the know-how. Here are my recomendations. Watch him ... he's very tricky,' was his advice before she left for Geneva.

Helga had heard a lot about Herman Rolfe as a man and as a tycoon, but she had no idea he was a cripple. She was a little shocked to find him walking with the aid of sticks and his skull-like face set in a sour grimace of pain. They had spent three hours together in Rolfe's luxury suite at the Bergues Hotel. At this meeting, Helga had been thirty-six years of age and outstandingly beautiful. She had poise and she understood men. She had brains and her added suggestions to the suggestions made by Archer impressed Rolfe.

Later, Archer had told her: 'You've made a hit with the old man ... he wants to see you again.'

Rolfe came to Switzerland a month later and to the office in Lausanne – something he hadn't done before. He had paused at Helga's desk and had shaken hands with her. 'Your suggestions were excellent,' he said, in his dry, harsh voice. 'Accept this as an appreciation.' He had given her a small package which contained a platinum and diamond wristwatch.

When he had gone, Archer called her into his office.

'The old man wants you to be his secretary. It's up to you, but I don't advise it.' He looked at her, smiling. 'Play your cards right and I have an idea you could become his wife. He's lonely, he wants someone to run his various homes, wants someone with brains, someone he can show off. You qualify. Want me to handle it?'

She stared at him. It took her several seconds to realize fully what he was saying, then she didn't hesitate.

'Do you think you can?'

'I'll bet on it.' He was excited. 'We've always got along together, darling. It would be a big thing for me to have you as his wife. We could work together. If you will marry him, I'll fix it.'

The wife of one of the richest men in the world! It was an irresistible thought at her age!

'Fix it, but I bet you don't!'

But Archer did.

Three months later, she had a letter from Rolfe asking her to meet him at the Montreux Palace hotel in Montreux and would she have dinner with him?

'This is it,' Archer told her. 'I've handed him to you on a plate. Lock the door, darling and get your pants off. I deserve a reward!'

Rolfe had been brisk and business-like. He explained he needed a wife. He had a number of homes dotted around Europe. He wanted someone to look after his place in Florida. He considered himself fortunate to have found her as she not only had looks, charm, poise but excellent brains. She was ideally fitted to become his wife. Would she accept him?

Helga knew coyness or hesitation would be the wrong approach. She looked straight at him.

'Yes. I hope I can give you as much as you are offering me.'

It was a reply that pleased him.

For a long uncomfortable minute, he studied her. His penetrating stare always made her feel uneasy, but now it really bothered her.

'I want to ask you a personal question before we make a final decision,' he said quietly. 'Does sex mean a lot to you?'

She had been shrewd enough to be expecting something like this and she was ready for it.

'Why do you ask?'

'I am a cripple,' Rolfe said. 'I am asking you if you are prepared to give up a normal sex life to become my wife. When we marry there must never be any other man ... never a breath of scandal. That is something I will not tolerate. If you cheat, Helga, I will divorce you and you will be left with nothing. Remember that. If you remain faithful to me, I will give you a fulfilled life. There are many compensations which I have discovered that can replace sex. If you are prepared to accept this condition, then we can be married as soon as I can make the arrangements.'

'I am thirty-six,' she replied. 'I have had all the sex I need.' At that moment, she believed what she was saying. 'I accept the condition.'

Of course it hadn't worked out like that. The first year was all right. The splendid Florida house, the excitement of being the wife of such a rich man, having everything she asked for, the people who swarmed around her made the sublimation of her sex urge comparatively easy. Then later when Helga got in with the clique of women who did nothing but talk about what their husbands did the previous night to them and the boy friends they had had on the sly, looking at her expectantly for her contribution, she began to suffer.

It was while driving to Milan on business for her husband, stopping at a small restaurant just outside the City that she made her first slip. There was a young Italian waiter, charming and sensual who seemed to know her need. When she went into the primitive toilet, he had followed her and had taken her, standing up and pressed against the none too clean wall. It had been dreadful and sordid that even now, four years in the past, she cringed to think of it.

This began a series of sexual adventures with strange men when the urge became unbearable. She was very careful. There were no affairs in Florida which was her husband's permanent home. It was only when she went to Europe on some mission to see Archer at her husband's request that she looked around for a likely male.

Apart from this occasional cheating, Helga gave Rolfe good service. He was busy planning new electronic marvels that would add to the progress of the world, add to his Empire and add to his fortune. He had told her he wanted her to work closely with Jack Archer. There were twenty million dollars invested in Switzerland.

'Keep the money turning over, Helga,' Rolfe said. 'You can do it. Let me have a six monthly report on what you and Archer are doing. This is your responsibility now ... don't forget, it is your money as much as mine.'

Archer's foresight was working out and Rolfe was delighted. The Rolfe fortune in Switzerland increased under their joint care. Her husband trusted her. He was thirty years older than she. She knew, eventually, she would inherit the bulk of his fortune. There was only a daughter from Rolfe's first marriage, but she presented no serious opposition. Rolfe never spoke of her. Helga got the idea that the girl had gone Hippy or something Anti and Rolfe had dismissed her from his mind. So eventually, she would inherit an enormous fortune and the world would be at her feet. But it depended on her discretion. *If you cheat, Helga, I will divorce you.* If ever he found out that she was cheating, she would lose everything he showered on her, but when the sexual urge seized her she couldn't resist it. She was like a demented woman playing Russian roulette.

She had this nagging desire to tell this boy, driving at her side, something about herself. It was just possible he might be interested ... might even be sympathetic. Not quite sure of him, glancing at his profile from time to time, she held back. Then after they had been driving for some time, she said abruptly, 'Because I have money and this car, you may think I have no problems.'

He started a little as if her voice surprised him. He was probably miles away in his thoughts, she thought bitterly. He had forgotten she was at his side.

'What was that, ma'am?'

She repeated what she had said.

'Yeah ... everyone has problems.' He nodded. 'Ron says problems are sent to us as a challenge.'

She thought: God! How bored I'm getting with Ron!

'It's not always easy to take up a challenge. I have a husband problem.'

He moved the Mercedes past a Fiat 125 with a gentle touch on the steering wheel, then he said, 'Is that right?'

There was no interest in his voice and she felt deflated and defeated.

'He is a cripple.'

'That's bad, ma'am.' Still no interest in his voice.

'It's hard on me.'

This time he turned to look at her, then switched his eyes back to the road.

'Yeah ... I can see that.'

'It can be lonely.'

'Sure.' He moved the car into the fast lane, overtaking three cars with a rush of speed that set her heart thumping. 'But I guess with your looks, ma'am, you needn't be all that lonely.'

She forced a laugh. 'I'm not lonely now, Larry.'

'Yeah.' He nodded frowning. 'Still a guy like me can't be much company for someone like you. I guess you're used to better talk. I don't reckon to be much of a talker.'

'I wouldn't have asked you along if I hadn't liked you.' She paused, then trying to take the pleading out of her voice, she asked, 'I hope you like me too.'

'Who wouldn't?' The conviction in his voice made her heart-beat quicken. 'Sure, I like you.'

If only he wasn't so young and if only he had a little more education and a little more brain. But he was beautiful, virile and wonderfully male. You can't expect too much, she told herself . . . count your blessings.

She began to ask him about himself and she learned his parents had a farm which provided them with a reasonable living and once this tour of Europe was over, he was going back to take over from his father.

'Will you like that Larry?'

He lifted his heavy shoulders.

'I guess. My old man is getting on and he needs me. I'm not good for much else.'

'Do you plan to marry?'

'I guess so, ma'am. You can't run a farm without a wife . . . that's what my old man says and I reckon he's right.'

'Is there a girl?'

'Not one particular one.'

'But there are girls?'

He shifted uneasily.

'Sure.'

Although she wanted to pursue this subject, she felt he might resent it. She told herself he couldn't be a virgin, but had he the experience to satisfy her? Regretfully, she switched to finding out his interests.

No, he didn't read . . . maybe the comics, but they bored him after a while. No, he didn't like classical music, but he dug for pop. He thought TV was a ball. No, he didn't follow politics. Nixon? He hadn't thought about Nixon. You had to have a President, so okay, you had a President. Sure he went to the movies. Yeah, he liked sexy films. He liked a good tough punch-up. He liked watching the fights on TV.

She listened, realizing the vast gap that lay between them.

Then suddenly, in front of them was a sign that said Basle was only thirty-five kilometres ahead of them.

'Basle? That's Switzerland, isn't it?' Larry said and there was a sudden change in his voice that made her look sharply at him.

'Yes.'

'That's the frontier . . . right?'

'Yes.'

He fingered his cap.

'What is it, Larry?'

'Nothing.' His voice had become curt and he slightly increased the speed of the car.

'But there is something . . . tell me.'

'Suppose we talk when we get to a parking, ma'am,' he said. The hard note in his voice frightened her. Why this sudden change? she asked herself, but feeling he would be irritated if she pressed for an immediate answer, she sat still, waiting.

Ten kilometres further along the autobahn, they came to a lay-by and he slowed, swung the car off the road and behind a thick hedge, covered with snow that hid a W.C. and stone tables and benches for the summer tourists.

He cut the engine, then half-turning in his seat, he looked directly at her.

'Ma'am, you told me about your problems, now it's my turn. I also have a problem.'

What was coming? she thought. What was he going to say?

'Well . . . Tell me,' she said, forcing her voice to sound normal.

'Well, ma'am, I told you I had lost my things and my money. I lost my passport too.'

She stared at him.

'You have no passport?'

'That's it.'

She tried to think efficiently, but she felt she wasn't succeeding.

'But have you reported losing it?'

'No, ma'am. Like I told you, I got mixed up in this Hamburg riot. The cops were looking for everyone mixed up in it. I had to get out fast.'

She sat still, trying to think. The German police at the frontier might let them through without checking passports, but the Swiss police on the far side of the barrier were certain to check. She tried to imagine how the Swiss police would react when Larry said he had lost his passport. She would get involved. Of course she could say she was giving him a ride, but that wouldn't help him. It would mean that she would lose him and this was something she was determined not to do.

'Why didn't you tell me before, Larry? I would have gone

29

with you to the American Consul at Bonn. We could have fixed it.'

He shook his head.

'It's not that simple, but it's okay. It can be fixed if you'll go along. Have you anything in the boot?'

She stiffened, staring at him.

'In the boot? My luggage ... what do you mean?'

'Do you want me to come with you to Switzerland?' he asked. 'I could be of help to you ... or maybe you don't want me?'

'I don't understand what you're saying ... what do you mean?'

'Look, ma'am, I have to get to the other side of the frontier. Ron told me where I can get a new passport. There's lots of ways to cross the frontier. If you don't want to help me, you say so. I'll leave you right here. I just thought as you've been so good to me, I'd like to stay with you if I can.' The warm brown eyes went over her face. 'There's no problem if you will help.'

She pressed her hand against her forehead.

'I don't understand.'

'I can go through the frontier in your boot, ma'am. It's no problem. Ron says they never look in the boot of a car owned by an American. They just wave you through.'

She thought back on the times she had been through the various frontiers. What he said was true. They had never looked in the boot ... maybe the Italians had, but then only once.

'But suppose they do find you?'

He grinned.

'Then it's my bad luck. You're in the clear, ma'am. If they find me, you know nothing about it. I'll tell them I found the boot unlocked and sneaked in when you were parking.'

'But they'll arrest you!'

'They won't find me, ma'am. Do you want to help me or don't you?'

What am I getting myself into? she wondered. If she refused he would go out of her life. Anyway, what had she to lose? As he had said, she could tell them she didn't know he was hiding in the boot.

'All right, Larry . . . go ahead.'

His face lit up.

'Thank you, ma'am. You won't regret this. You take over.' He slid out of the car and went around to the back. She moved into the driving seat and watched him in the driving mirror transfer her cases to the back seat.

He came to the driver's window and smiled at her.

'Take it easy, ma'am . . . there'll be no problem.'

She forced a smile.

'I hope not, Larry.'

He gave her the thumbs up sign, then went around to the back. She waited until she heard the lid of the boot slam shut, then bracing herself, she drove the car back on to the autobahn.

CHAPTER TWO

A FEW kilometres before the German frontier, Helga ran
into a blinding snowstorm. She had been driving along the
autobahn in reasonable light when suddenly it turned dark,
and as she switched on the headlights, snow, whipped by the
wind, blotted out visibility to within twenty metres.

The cars ahead of her, now crawling, quickly turned into
white mounds of snow: their red tail lights scarcely visible.
In spite of having to drive under these difficult conditions,
Helga was thankful. From past experience, she knew the
frontier guards were cursory in their check when the
weather was this bad.

Her mind was in a daze of bewilderment, excitement and
doubt. She had read and heard so much about the dangers of
picking up a lone hitch hiker, but this boy had seemed so
open, friendly and warm. She had been convinced he was
completely honest and likeable, but now she began to
wonder. Was it really possible he could have lost everything,
including his passport? But he was honest, she assured herself. He had wanted to return the money she had given
him. This business about having to get into Switzerland
and this man Ron he had told him about from whom he could
get another passport (forged?) really worried her. She
remembered the conviction in Larry's voice when he
had said, *Sure, I like you.* No one could speak like that
without meaning it, but all the same, was he making use
of her?

She saw the frontier sign with the word HALT, half
hidden by the snow. The cars ahead of her were already
crawling by the frontier post. She could see the German
guard, snug behind his glass shelter, waving them impatiently through.

Her heart was thumping when it came to her turn, but the

guard merely waved his hand and then turned away. She had her passport and green card on her lap. Now for the Swiss frontier, she thought and flinched. She was behind three cars. Two of them were waved through: the one just ahead of her had Swiss number plates. She felt a chill of fear when she saw two frontier guards, their capes and peaked caps covered with snow, standing either side of the car ahead. There was some talk, then the guard on the off-side of the car came towards her. She lowered the window, seeing the Swiss car move off.

The guard saluted her, his face purple with the cold and accepted her passport and green card.

As he flicked through the pages of her passport, he asked, 'Have you anything to declare?'

'No, nothing.'

She realized he was looking at her and there was approval in his eyes and she forced a smile.

He returned her papers.

'Have you heard if it is getting worse?' she asked.

'It couldn't be worse than this, madame,' he said with a grin, then he saluted her and stepped back.

She wound up the window and set the car moving. She felt a little sick but triumphant. Now she had the problem of getting Larry out of the boot. She couldn't just stop and let him get out to be seen by any and every eye.

He must be freezing in the boot, she thought as she drove with the traffic. Then ahead of her she saw a big building site. In this blizzard, no one could be working, she thought and she swung the car on to the rough road leading to the site. Looking in the driving mirror she saw she had already lost sight of the main road, wiped from view by the blinding snow. She stopped the car, got out into the driving snow and ran around to the boot. She had to struggle to release the catch, then she lifted the lid.

'Quick!'

He slid out and had shut the boot before she realized he was moving.

'You drive ... I'll tell you where to go,' she said and ran around to the passenger's seat.

They both got in the car and slammed the doors, then she

found him looking at her, his face alight with that warm, friendly grin.

'You see, ma'am ... like I told you ... it worked.'

'Yes ... you must be frozen.'

'I'm fine, but I want to thank you, ma'am.' He reached out and his hand closed over hers. 'I really appreciate it and I think you have a load of guts if you'll excuse me saying it like that.'

She could feel his coldness through her glove.

'Let's get something to eat,' she said reluctantly withdrawing her hand. 'Then we can talk.'

She directed him up St. Jacobs strasse, then she told him to turn right where there was a parking lot. As he found space and cut the engine, he said, 'You know this town, ma'am?'

'I know it. There's a restaurant not far from here. We'll have to walk. Would you put my suitcases in the boot?'

Ten minutes later, both plastered with snow, they entered the steam heat of a modest restaurant she had once visited on another of her lone journeys.

Because she was not only cold but very nervous she could face nothing but a plate of soup. She ordered soup, two large pork chops and chips for Larry.

'Let's eat first,' she said, sure he would be interested only in the food that was coming and wouldn't concentrate on answering her questions.

When the meal was finished and they had thawed out and were sipping coffee, she said, 'Look, Larry, I want to know more about this. I want to know more about this girl who took your passport.'

He looked away and she imagined he was shuffling his feet.

'Well, ma'am, I guess you've done enough for me for me to lay it on the line, but I guess it's kind of embarrassing.' He stared down at his hands, frowning. 'You see, ma'am, every so often I have to have a woman.' He pulled at the peak of his cap. This time she hadn't reminded him to take it off. 'I get this urge, and it gets too much for me.' Again he dragged at the peak of his cap. 'Excuse me. You asked me ... I'm laying it on the line. I hope you will understand.'

34

Yes, I understand, she thought, you get this urge from time to time. I'm never free of it!

'Of course, Larry . . . was she a pro?'

He nodded, not looking at her.

'Yeah. It got pretty hairy. Two guys broke in, and there was a punch-up. They sure handled me and they threw me out.' He looked at her, then away. 'I guess I was lucky to keep my trousers.'

She searched his face for any signs of a fight, but found none. She felt compassion. She understood he didn't want to admit to her that some cheap little whore had robbed him of everything he owned.

There was no point in pressing this, she decided. It really wasn't important. He was just a kid . . . kids did things like this. The important thing was his passport.

'Well, Larry, we are now in Switzerland,' she said. 'You have no passport. What are you going to do?'

'I guess I've got to have a passport.' He fingered the peak of his cap, then he flushed. 'Goddamn it! I'm still wearing this goddamn thing!' He tore the cap off his head and stuffed it under his thigh. 'Excuse me, ma'am. I guess I'm a hick. I just don't know when I'm wearing it.'

'How do you get another passport?' she asked. 'What was this you said about . . . Ron?'

He shifted in his seat.

'Well, he gave me an address right here, ma'am. It costs, but I can get around to that.' He leaned forward, resting his big hands on the table and looked directly at her. 'Look, ma'am, you've done enough for me. Thank you for everything. Thank you for getting me through the frontier. Thank you for this meal. You've been great! Now, I'm on my own. From now on, you don't have to think of me. I'll manage.'

She regarded him steadily.

'That was a very pretty speech, Larry, but I think you have been watching too much television. Your next line, set against a fading sunset should be, "And thanks for the memory, but this is goodbye".'

He turned beetroot red as he gaped at her.

'What was that again, ma'am?'

She took from her bag her gold cigarette case and lit a cigarette with her gold Dunhill.

'I go so far, Larry, but don't push it. I don't kid easily. If you want to be on your own, then get up and go. If you want to manage on your own so bravely, I'm not stopping you, but don't give me this corny dialogue ... do I make myself clear?'

He reached for the peak of his cap, but not finding it, he ran his fingers through his hair.

'Excuse me, ma'am. I didn't mean a come-on. Honest ... I'm just a hick ... excuse me.'

She sat still, her eyes cold and searching as she regarded him.

'If you want to be on your own, Larry, get up right now and get out of here!'

He flinched, then rubbed his chin with the back of his hand and she could see sweat beads forming on his forehead.

'I don't want to go, ma'am ... excuse me.'

'All right, but don't ever try to con me again, Larry,' she said quietly. 'I know it all. I've seen it all. While you were feeding the hens, I was in the middle of a jungle where men with fifty times your brain-power were cutting each other's throat. The biggest throat cutter of them all was and still is my husband. Let's get this straight. I like you ... you're a nice refreshing kid, but don't try to con me.'

He nodded.

'I didn't mean to ... honest, ma'am.'

'All right. Now tell me what your friend told you about getting a passport.'

Unhappily and without much hope, he tried to reassert his manhood.

'It's okay, ma'am. I can manage.'

She leaned forward.

'Isn't it time you realized you can no more manage without me than you could have changed your nappy when you were three months old?'

He hung his head and she could see the depressed misery on his face.

'I guess you're right, ma'am. That sure is laying it on the line. Yeah ... I guess you're right.'

'We don't have to make a drama out of this,' she said. 'What's this about your passport?'

'I can get a new passport in a new name. There's a guy here in Basle who can fix it. I have his address right here,' and he tapped his shirt pocket.

'Why do you have to have a *new* name, Larry? Why can't you go to the American Consul and tell them your passport has been stolen?'

He said nothing, but stared down at the table and the sweat beads on his forehead grew to drops and began to trickle down his face.

'Larry! I'm asking you a question!'

He looked up miserably.

'I guess the cops are looking for me.'

She felt a little jolt under her heart.

'Why?'

'It was this riot, ma'am. I told you it got rough. A guy right with me hit a cop with a brick, then he scrammed. Two other cops grabbed me. This cop had a bust nose. I told them I didn't do it, but they didn't believe me. They took my passport and started lugging me to the wagon when Ron turned up and rescued me. He told me to scram ... so I scrammed.'

'So this tart didn't steal your passport?'

'That's right, ma'am, but she took everything else.'

She lit another cigarette while she thought.

'So the German police have your passport and they are looking for you ... is that right?'

'That's right, ma'am.'

She told herself: What I should do now is to pay the check, walk out and leave him. But because her body was yearning for him, she immediately dismissed this solution.

'You wouldn't be lying to me, Larry?' she asked. 'Be careful! I want the truth.'

He wiped his sweating face with the back of his hand, then looking at her, he shook his head.

'Swear to God, ma'am.'

She regarded him.

'Does God mean anything to you?'

He stiffened.

'Why, sure . . . God is God.'

She lifted her shoulders. She didn't really care if he was lying or not. God is God . . . how simple it was to say that. Again she felt the hot blood move tormentingly down to her loins.

'Tell me about the passport. Who is this man?'

'I have his address right here.' He took a scrap of paper from his shirt pocket and pushed it across the table. 'He's a friend of Ron.' He hesitated, then went on, 'It costs three thousand francs.'

Three thousand francs!

'You're becoming a little expensive, aren't you, Larry?' She looked at the typewritten address. The man's name was Max Friedlander. The address meant nothing to her.

'Look, ma'am, I'll manage. I'll find a job. . .'

'Oh, stop it! We'll go together and we'll get the passport.'

He looked uneasily at her.

'I wouldn't want you to get involved. You've already been too good for me. If you really mean to help, then give me the money and I'll get it fixed.'

'If you imagine I am going to give you three thousand francs without being certain how you spend it, you need your head examined,' she said curtly.

She signalled to the waiter. As she was paying the check she asked him where the street was, written on the paper.

The waiter went away and returned with a street map and showed her exactly where to find the street. She slid him a tip that made his eyes widen, then she put on her wet mink coat and left the restaurant.

His shoulders hunched against the driving snow, Larry followed her.

Max Friedlander had a ground-floor apartment in a shabby block in a derelict-looking courtyard.

Plastered with snow and very cold, Helga looked at the name plate screwed to the door.

'This is it,' she said.

Larry took off his cap and shook the snow from it, replaced it and read the name plate.

38

'Yeah. Look, ma'am, I don't want you to get involved. I guess . . .'

'Oh, stop it! We've gone over that part of the script before,' Helga said impatiently and she rang the bell.

There was a delay while they stood in the steadily falling snow, then the door opened. A small, shadowy man stood in the doorway. There was a dim yellow light at the end of the passage that made more shadows.

'What is it? Who is it?' The voice was a little shrill and very querulous.

A pansy! Helga thought. She loathed the breed, and she moved forward, pressing the man back, determined to get out of the falling snow.

'Mr. Friedlander?'

'Yes . . . yes. What is it? You're making a mess on my floor!'

'Larry . . . talk to him,' Helga said, an edge to her voice.

Larry moved past her, snow dropping from his shoulders. His big body blocked the little man from her sight. She heard him say softly, 'Ron Smith told me to come.'

'Well, shut the door for pity's sake! Look at the mess you're making!'

Helga closed the door, then because she already hated this little man, she shook the snow off her coat and taking off her hat, shook that too making a snow puddle on the floor.

Larry had moved forward. Now a door opened and a brighter light came out into the narrow, dimly lit passage.

Welcome heat came from the room and she moved in. The room was shabbily furnished with heavy antique, knocked about furniture. On the table stood a silver pheasant. Looking around, Helga decided this was the only good piece in the room and she would have liked to have owned it. She could now see this man more clearly as he stood under the light coming from an ornate chandelier: only three of its many electric lights functioning.

He was around sixty years of age. His pinched, sallow-complexioned face wore the marks of suffering. His black eyes had the cunning of a cornered fox. His lank grey hair sprouted from under a black beret. Wearing a soiled polo-necked green sweater and a shapeless pair of green corduroy

39

trousers, he looked dirty and she saw his fingernails were long and black.

'Ronnie told you to come? How do I know?' he said, looking at Larry.

'Ron said Gilly thinks of you . . . he said you would know what that means.'

Friedlander squirmed with pleasure and giggled. Watching him, Helga hated him.

'Yes, I know . . . how is Ronnie?'

'Right now he is in jail.'

Friedlander nodded.

'I saw it in the papers, Ronnie's smart. Did they hurt him?'

'No.'

'That's good.' A long pause while the three looked at each other, then Friedlander said, 'What can I do for you, dear? Any friend of Ronnie's my friend.'

'I want a passport,' Larry said. 'One of your specials.'

Friedlander's foxy eyes shifted to Helga.

'Who is your friend, dear?'

'I'm the one who is paying for it,' Helga said. 'That's all you need know.'

Friedlander's eyes took in her mink coat and her hat. Then his eyes shifted to her lizard skin bag and he smiled.

'You got photographs, dear?'

Larry groped in his hip pocket and brought out a soiled envelope.

'All the dope's here.'

'It will be four thousand five hundred francs,' Friedlander said as he took the envelope. 'Cash down and a beautiful job . . . it's cheap at the price.'

The old come-on, Helga thought and looked at Larry who was staring at Friedlander. I'll give him a chance, but if he can't handle it, then I will.

'Ron said it would be three.' She was pleased to hear Larry's voice sounded firm.

Friedlander lifted his dirty hands with a shrug of regret.

'Dear Ron . . . he isn't keeping pace with the rising cost of living. It's now four thousand five, and it'll be a beautiful job.'

40

'Ron said I shouldn't pay more than three,' Larry said.

'So sorry ... Ron isn't with it any more.' The smile, foxy and shifty moved from Larry to Helga.

'That's too bad,' Larry said. 'We don't pay more than three.'

'Goodbye,' Friedlander said, waving to the door. 'When you see Ronnie again, tell him my price has gone up.'

'I don't have too,' Larry said. 'Ronnie told me something. He said you were a great artist.' He leaned forward to peer at Friedlander. 'What would it cost you if you got your hands crushed in a door?'

Helga stiffened, feeling a chill move up her spine. She looked at Larry. He seemed the same friendly, gum chewing boy, but this new note in his voice told her his threat was genuine.

Friedlander stared at Larry, then he took a quick step back.

'What are you saying?'

'Are you deaf? I want the passport, buster and I'm not paying more than three.' Larry was chewing gum and he seemed mild and friendly. 'Do we make a deal or do I feed your fingers in the door?'

Friedlander's face showed terror. His back was now against the wall.

'I'll do it for three,' he said huskily. 'I wouldn't do it for anyone else.'

'I'm not asking you to do it for anyone else,' Larry said. 'Go ahead ... we'll wait.'

Friedlander shifted his feet.

'I would like the money first.'

'We'll wait,' Larry repeated.

Friedlander looked hopefully at Helga.

'Can I rely on you to pay me?'

'I'll pay you,' Helga said and went to a chair and sat down.

Friedlander looked at her, then at Larry, then he went out of the room, closing the door behind him.

There was a long pause, then Helga said, 'You handled that rather well, Larry.'

He pulled at the peak of his cap.

'Thank you, ma'am. It was your money. You've been generous enough to me. I couldn't let you get gypped.'

'Thank you.' She regarded him. 'That was quite a thought ... about crushing his hands in the door. Would you have done it?'

Again he pulled at his cap, shaking his head.

'No, ma'am. I don't believe in hurting people.'

Again she looked at him, remembering the note in his voice that had sent a chill up her spine. Was he really such a warm, friendly simple boy as he seemed?

'How am I going to pay him?' she asked suddenly. 'I have only Traveller's cheques. While we are waiting, I'd better find a bank.'

He crossed to the window, lifted the dirty curtain and looked out at the steadily falling snow.

'You can't go out in this. Couldn't you pay it into his bank?'

'I don't want him to know my name.'

He turned and looked at her, nodding.

'Yeah ... there's that.' He hesitated, frowning. 'You've done enough for me. I ...'

'All right, Larry, I know what I'm doing for you. I don't have to be reminded.' She got to her feet. 'I'll find a bank. You wait here,' and she went out into the passage and to the front door. She hoped he would have come after her, but he didn't. Shrugging, she pulled her coat around her and went out into the falling snow.

As she looked for a bank, she wondered if she shouldn't go back to where the Mercedes was parked and drive away. She had a growing conviction that by remaining with this boy she was building a complication around herself that she was going to regret.

But she found a bank at the end of the street and she cashed five thousand dollars into Swiss francs which she stuffed into her bag. Coming out of the bank, she looked to the left, knowing, not far away, the Mercedes was waiting under a blanket of snow. She hesitated only for a few seconds. She was lonely and needed a man. She walked to the right, and in five minutes she was knocking on Friedlander's front door.

42

Larry opened the door.

'Is it all right, ma'am?' he asked, standing aside to let her in.

'It's all right.' She walked into the shabby living-room, feeling the heat seeping through her. 'How long do you think we will have to wait?'

'I don't know, ma'am.' He closed the door and leaned against it, his big hands thrust into the pockets of his jeans. His jaw moved rhythmically as he chewed.

She took off her coat and hung it over a chair, then she sat down. 'We can't hope to go further today in this blizzard. We'd better find an hotel.'

'We can go on if you want to, ma'am. I'm used to driving in the snow.'

She looked at her watch. The time was 15.15. She yearned for the luxury of the Adlon hotel. She longed to sink into a hot, relaxing bath and then rest on a bed until dinner time. She realized she couldn't take Larry to the hotel, looking the way he did and without luggage. She was well known there. Then she remembered passing a store on her way to the bank.

She made an instant, impulsive decision.

'Listen, Larry, I don't want to go on. I want to rest. You can't come with me to an hotel, dressed as you are.' She opened her bag and took out some Swiss money. 'There is a store at the end of the street: turn right as you leave here. I want you to buy yourself a dark suit, a white shirt and black tie. You will also need a lined mackintosh and shoes. You will come to the hotel as my chauffeur. Please take this money and buy these things. Will you also change at the store? Put what you have on in a suitcase.'

He was staring blankly at her.

'But I can't do that, ma'am. It wouldn't be right. I . . .'

'Oh, for God's sake do as I ask!' Her voice had become waspish. 'I'm tired! There's the money . . . do what I say!'

Startled by the note in her voice, he picked up the money, pulled at the peak of his cap, then went out. She heard the front door slam.

She drew in a long breath, then with unsteady hands, she lit a cigarette. She waited, aware of the uncanny silence that

43

hung over the building. She was getting more and more involved, she thought, but this was something that had happened before in a different way. In her present mood, she accepted risks.

In an hour or so, she thought, she would be at the hotel where the service was perfect. She imagined getting into the bath, resting in the bed and then, drinking her first vodka martini. The hotel would accept Larry as her chauffeur, but she would have to be careful. He would have to eat on his own and this she regretted – how bored she was eating meals alone in luxury restaurants, but she knew the hotel would raise its eyebrows and remember if Mrs. Herman Rolfe took dinner with her chauffeur. But after dinner, when she was in the seclusion of her bedroom, she would telephone to Larry, telling him to come to her. He was almost certain to be a clumsy, selfish lover, but she would control him. Her heart began to hammer as she imagined the moment when he took her roughly in his arms.

The door opened, startling her and Friedlander came in. He looked around, his cunning little eyes puzzled.

'Where's Larry?'

'He'll be back. Have you got it?'

'Of course.' He edged into the room, closing the door. 'It's a beautiful job.'

'Let me see it.'

He hesitated, then coming over to her, he handed her the passport. It looked genuine enough and was just worn enough to be acceptable. The name on the passport was Larry Sinclair. Profession: Student. Larry a student? She shrugged. The word Student meant nothing these days: a smoke screen behind which so many young people hid as the word Model was used as often as a smoke screen for a whore.

The photograph was poor, but the stamp looked authentic.

'Yes ... it is good.'

'It is a work of art,' Friedlander said peevishly. 'It is worth more than three thousand. Be fair, dear ... give me another five hundred. That's not being unreasonable.'

She opened her bag and without taking the roll of money

44

from the bag, she stripped off three one thousand franc bills and dropped them on to the table. Then she put the passport in her bag and closed it.

'If you want more, talk to Larry,' she said.

He picked up the bills and put them in his pocket.

'Don't make mistakes, dear ... so easy to make mistakes.' He stared at her. 'Meanness always comes home to roost.'

She eyed him with contempt.

'Go away! You and your filthy breed bore me!'

His small eyes turned baleful.

'Don't say I didn't warn you.' He backed to the door. 'I'd rather be what I am than what you are,' and he flounced out of the room.

She sat still, furious, and then after thinking, she suddenly became sick of herself. His parting shot had hurt.

Twenty minutes later, Larry returned. She heard him tap on the front door and she went to open it. He came in out of the falling snow and into the light of the shabby room. She scarcely recognized him. Gone was the gum chewing hick American. The black tie and the white collar completely changed his appearance. The black trench coat was as formal as a uniform. He looked like the chauffeur of the wealthy owner of a Mercedes 300SEL. He was carrying a cheap plastic suitcase and he looked anxiously at her, seeking her approval.

'Wonderful, Larry,' she said, smiling at him. 'You look splendid.'

He grinned boyishly.

'I got what you told me, ma'am.'

'Yes ... I have your passport ... let's go.'

'I picked up the car, ma'am.' He eyed her a little doubtfully. 'It's right outside. Excuse me for the liberty ... I didn't think you would want to walk all that way to the parking lot.'

She stared at him.

'But how could you? I have the ignition key!'

He automatically reached for the peak of his cap, then finding he wasn't wearing the cap, he rubbed his forehead with the back of his hand.

'I'm used to cars, ma'am. I don't need ignition keys. Excuse me if I did wrong.'

'But the car was locked!'

'Yes ... that's right. I just thought I'd save you the walk. It's snowing pretty hard out there.'

A feeling of fear ran through her. It passed in a moment as she realized how she would have hated to have trudged through the thick snow to the car. He's clever! she thought. Not only clever, but considerate!

'Thank you for being so thoughtful,' she said and smiled at him. She opened her bag and handed him the ignition key. 'In spite of your cleverness, perhaps you better have this.'

He opened the front door and together they went to where he had parked the car. He opened the off-side door and she slid in. Then he went around to the driver's seat, paused to shake the snow off his new black shoes, then dropped into the driver's seat.

She told him how to get to the Adlon hotel.

'You gave me too much money, ma'am,' he said as he edged the car out of the courtyard. 'I have the change.'

'That's all right, Larry. You'll need some spending money ... keep it.'

He shook his head.

'No, ma'am, thank you. I explained before ... I don't accept money.'

She smiled at him.

'All right, Larry ... I understand. We'll settle up when we get to the hotel.'

She relaxed back, thinking: He is really rather sweet.

As he drove with the traffic, the wipers swishing away the snow, she looked searchingly at his profile, lit by the passing street lamps, and again she felt a rush of hot blood go through her.

When Helga, followed by Larry, followed by a porter carrying her bags, entered the reception lobby of the Adlon hotel, Karl Fock, the owner of the hotel, happened to be making one of his rare appearances. He immediately recognized her as one of the hotel's most valued guests.

Karl Fock was built in a generous style. He reminded Helga of the late, unlamented Herman Göering. Fock believed that by snapping his fingers, the world instantly became his oyster, and within his limited sphere, the world did become his oyster. His welcome was warm and slightly overpowering. He bowed over Helga's hand, brushing her glove with his thick, moist lips. In a loud guttural voice that carried across the lobby, he declared his happiness to see her again. He had the best suite ready for her. He would conduct her there in person.

The lobby was full of American and Japanaese tourists who stopped their chatter to stare. Helga became the centre of attaction. She was flattered as she became engulfed by Fock's warm welcome. She was also flattered to see the three reception clerks were bowing to her, ignoring all other guests.

She looked behind her and caught Larry's eyes. He looked completely bewildered, but Fock snatched her attention away.

'What a wonderful welcome,' she said, her smile stiff. 'I have a chauffeur ... er ... what ...?'

A chauffeur?

Fock's heavy black eyebrows climbed. His expression conveyed that a chauffeur was something of no importance, but seeing her concern, he spun around and snapped his fingers. In dismay, Helga saw the bewildered looking Larry whisked out of sight by a bowing lackey.

Tired, bemused and a little overwhelmed, Helga allowed herself to be escorted to the elevator.

The suite into which she was bowed was the best in the hotel.

'Madame Rolfe, you are exhausted,' Fock said, standing just inside the room. 'A maid will unpack for you. Please rest. I would so much like to hear news of Mr. Rolfe. Would you give me the pleasure of dining with me? Please don't disappoint me.'

Helga hesitated, then she forced a smile. It was impossible to refuse, although dinner with Karl Fock was the last thing she wanted.

'I shall be delighted. You are very kind.'

A fat, comfortable looking maid appeared in the doorway.

'It will be my pleasure,' Fock said, bowing. 'Then at eight-thirty?'

'Yes.' She hesitated. 'My chauffeur?'

Fock waved his fat hands.

'Madame ... don't worry about anything.' He showed his white teeth that resembled the keys of a piano and was gone.

But she did worry, wondering what was happening to Larry. The maid, fat, slow and kind, irritated her. She wanted to telephone down to the reception desk and find out just what they were doing with Larry, but with the maid in the room, she felt it would be indiscreet. She was sure Larry was being taken care of, but she did want to know how he was reacting.

The maid made a great fuss about drawing the bath, but eventually she left. Helga longed to get into the bath, but she hesitated by the telephone. Would it cause the hotel's eyebrows to lift if she inquired after her chauffeur? Because she had an uneasy conscience, she moved away from the telephone. She had to be careful, she told herself, and yet, she longed to know what was happening to Larry.

After lying in the hot, scented bath for some twenty minutes, she dried herself, put on a black chiffon wrap and lay on the vast bed. She looked at the wall clock. The time was 18.10. She stretched herself like a relaxing cat, spreading her beautiful legs and then cupping her heavy, firm breasts in her hands. If only Larry would walk into the room and take her, she thought. She closed her eyes, releasing her mind into an erotic dream.

She came awake by a gentle tapping on the door. Startled, she looked at the wall clock. The time now was 19.30. pulling her wrap around her, she called to come in. Could it be Larry? Her heart beat quickened.

The sight of the waiter who came in, carrying a frosted cocktail shaker and a glass which he placed on the table with a flourish sent her heart beat practically down to zero.

'With Herr Director's compliments, madame,' he said and poured from the shaker.

When he had gone, she drank the vodka martini gratefully, then, seeing the time was slipping by, she began to dress. While she slapped lotion on her face, then arranged her eyelashes, she thought of Larry. After the second vodka martini which was very strong, she was sufficiently nerved to telephone the reception desk.

'This is Madame Rolfe ... what have you done with my chauffeur?'

'Madame Rolfe?' The voice became servile. 'Your chauffeur? A moment, please.'

There was a pause and she could hear whispering voices and she regretted asking. This was a stupid, dangerous thing to have done. Why should a woman in her position ask after her chauffeur? Well, she had done it, now she would have to carry it off.

'Madame Rolfe?' A new voice, even more ingratiating.

'Yes.'

'Your chauffeur is in room 556. He will have dinner with the staff. Is that satisfactory?'

Staff? What did that mean? But she didn't have the courage to ask.

'Yes ... thank you,' and she hung up.

Because she was ashamed of her cowardice, she had a third vodka martini and by the time she had finished dressing, she was slightly drunk. She paused before the mirror at the door of the suite and surveyed herself. She was pleased with her reflection. She was really remarkable, she told herself. At the age of forty (forty-three?) she was slim and lovely to look at and immaculately dressed. She knew, as most women know who accept the truth, that she was still attractive to any man.

Karl Fock was waiting for her in the cocktail bar. In the haze of two more vodka martinis and rather overpowered by his guttural voice, Larry slipped from her mind. She remembered him as Fock escorted her into the restaurant but forgot him again when she was enveloped by the Maître d'hotel and three of his satellites and then the Chef, in his white cap and coverall, who bowed, beamed and shook hands with her while the rest of the guests in the restaurant stared, whispered and envied.

The dinner was impeccable: Belon oysters and a Chablis: a plump partridge and a 1959 Petur.

She heard herself talking. No, her husband wasn't too well, but he planned to be in Basle next year (A lie). Yes, the drive from Bonn had been bad, but there had been no ice on the autobahn. Yes, of course, she was delighted to be back in her favourite City (A lie). Her chauffeur? This question was unexpected and for a moment she lost her poise, then she smiled, shrugged her beautiful shoulders. Yes ... something new, but her husband wanted someone to drive her. She looked into Fock's moist, admiring eyes and she pulled a comic grimace. Husbands get fussy. She preferred to drive herself. But husbands! She laughed, and Fock was enchanted. Yes, this new chauffeur seemed very capable. He had been recommended ... an American student ... very serious.

Tired of being questioned, she switched the conversation to Fock's wife (a gruesome bore) and to his children (monsters).

Fock insisted on champagne with the sorbet and Helga was pretty drunk by the time coffee and brandy were served.

She made a charming little speech of thanks at the end of the meal, and then allowed herself to be escorted to her room.

Thankfully, she got rid of Fock at her bedroom door, then she walked a little unsteadily to her bed and dropped on to it.

She had been spoilt. It had been a wonderful reception. It had been a wonderful meal. Bore though he was, Fock had been kind to her. Now, to complete a perfect evening, she wanted Larry. She wanted this primitive boy to use her as he must have used the stupid, giggling girls on his farm. She wanted to be bruised, violently used, even beaten if that was what he liked, but she wanted him ... how she wanted him!

Getting off the bed, she threw off her clothes, tossing her dress, her bra, her pants, her stockings from her until she was naked.

Drunk, excited, she stood in the middle of the bedroom, her hands cupping her breasts, feeling the stabbing need for a man tormenting her. She imagined the scene in another

few minutes. She had to be careful not to be too blatant ...
not to shock him. She would have on her chiffon wrap.
When he came into the room, she would look at him ... a
long pause ... then a smile. Then, when he had closed the
door, she would go to him. She was sure he would read from
her smile the green light to go ahead and he would take her.
She hoped he wouldn't turn shy. It was possible he might be
too scared of her to take what she was offering, but she
thought that couldn't be possible.

With her heart beating fast, she picked up the telephone
receiver.

'Give me room 556, please.'

'Certainly madame ... a moment, please.'

Helga grimaced. Of course the girl knew who she was
speaking to. The slight flustered note in her voice told her
that.

There was a long pause, then the girl said, 'I'm sorry,
madame, there is no reply.'

No reply! Helga's fingers tightened on the receiver. Surely
he couldn't be asleep already? She looked at the wall clock.
It was 22.35.

'Try again!' she was immediately sorry for allowing her
voice to sound so harsh.

'Yes, madame.' Again a long pause, then the girl said, 'I'm
very sorry, madame, but there is still no reply.'

Helga drew in a long, slow breath. Only with an effort, she
kept control of her temper.

'Give me the reception desk!'

There was another infuriating delay, then the Reception
Manager came on the line. During the wait, Helga guessed
the girl had alerted him. When he answered, there was a
bow in his voice.

'Madame Rolfe? Is there anything I can do?'

'I want to speak to my chauffeur.'

'Your chauffeur?' There was a slight lift in his voice of
surprise. She thought bitterly, if she had asked to be connected to God he might have been less surprised. 'Of course,
madame ... please, a moment.'

She sat on the bed, feeling the sensual warmth of her body
evaporating.

51

'Madame?' The voice came back on the line.

'Well?' She knew the snap in her voice was unfortunate, but she couldn't control it.

'Your chauffeur has gone out. He left an hour ago. Is there anything I can do?'

'He has gone out?' A mistake, Helga thought, but she couldn't keep the words back.

'Did you want him, madame?' The bowing voice took on a worried note.

Do you want him? Helga's body ached. How I want him!

'No . . . it isn't important.' Slowly she replaced the receiver.

She got off the bed and walked to the window. She pulled aside the drapes and looked down at the busy street. The snow had stopped falling. The trams clanged and sparks flew from the overhead cables. People, in furs, walked carefully over the frozen snow. She let the drapes drop and went over to the bed and slipped on the chiffon wrap. She felt cold and now she wished she hadn't drunk so much.

It was her own fault, she told herself. She hadn't given him the slightest hint that she wanted him to come to her room. But where had he gone?

She dropped on to the bed, staring up at the ceiling.

Had he got this urge he had told her about . . . the urge that was now crucifying her? Had he gone out into the cold and the snow in search of some cheap little whore when she was here, in luxury and warmth, longing for him?

She lay there, her mind tormented, then after a while, she began to weep.

CHAPTER THREE

From a drugged sleep, Helga came awake at 08.00. She turned on the bedside lamp and then lay still, staring up at the ceiling. Thank God, she thought, for sleeping pills!

Making the effort, she picked up the telephone receiver.

'Coffee, please. Please tell my chauffeur I will be leaving at nine o'clock. Have my account ready,' and she replaced the receiver.

As she got out of bed she thought what a fool she would look if they called back to tell her her chauffeur was missing. It was possible Larry had walked out on her ... he might even have taken her car! Then she told herself to be realistic. She had his passport. Anyway, why should she doubt him? Last night had been her fault. She hadn't given him the slightest hint she wanted him to make love to her.

She hated the sight of herself as she looked in the bathroom mirror, but she wasn't dismayed. She was an expert at repairing damage.

After drinking two cups of coffee and after using every guile in her make-up box, she again looked in the mirror and this time she nodded her approval.

There came a tap on the door. She slipped on her mink coat, picked up her hat and opened the door.

The manager of the hotel, behind him a porter, bowed with a smile.

'Your car is waiting, madame.'

Together they went in the elevator to the reception lobby. Because she knew it was expected of her, she said how well she had slept and how pleased she had been with the room.

Beaming his pleasure, the manager escorted her to the desk and a bowing clerk slid the account across the polished wood. After glancing at the total, she paid. As the clerk was changing her Travellers' cheques she looked more closely at the bill.

An item caught her eye.

'What is this? A call to Hamburg?'

The clerk looked at the account, then at her and his expression became worried.

'Yes, madame. Your chauffeur made the call.'

Fifteen francs! It must have been a long call, she thought.

'Of course . . . I was forgetting.'

She picked up her change, shook hands with the clerk, saying she would see him next year, then, escorted by the manager, watched by a group of tourists, waiting for their bus, she went out into the cold where the Mercedes was parked.

Larry was standing by the car. She looked quickly at him. He gave her his warm, friendly smile as he opened the offside door. The porter put her bags into the boot and she tipped him. The manager, his nose now blue with the cold, still managed to keep a bright smile on his face. She shook hands with him, slid into the passenger's seat while Larry ran around the car and got in under the wheel.

There were more bows, then Larry moved the car into the traffic.

'Morning, ma'am,' he said, his voice cheerful.

'You turn right at the end of the street, then straight ahead,' Helga said, her voice cold and hostile.

'Sure, ma'am, I know the way, I got it all figured out on a map.'

'That was very clever of you.'

The snap in her voice wasn't lost on him and he looked quickly at her.

'Are you okay, ma'am?'

'I have a headache. Would you please keep quiet?'

'Sure, ma'am . . . is there anything I can do?'

'Just keep quiet.'

She knew she was behaving badly and she realized looking at him, that her petulance had made no impression on him. She saw him give a slight shrug, then he concentrated on his driving. She was irritated that he was so efficient, getting

54

them through the Basle traffic with ease and then on to the autobahn to Zurich. She had always hated this part of the drive and often she had made a mistake.

Determined to sulk, she smoked cigarette after cigarette in silence, staring at the broad road as it came towards her. She had done this run so often, it bored her. But finally, as they approached the outskirts of Zurich, she said, 'Do you know the way through the City?'

'Sure, ma'am,' he said calmly. 'Right ahead, forking left at the traffic lights, through the tunnel and on to the Chur by-pass.'

'That's right.'

She looked at him. He was chewing gum and his face was completely relaxed. She looked at his big hands on the steering-wheel and again her body melted in desire for him.

It wasn't until they had begun to climb the twisting road to Chur that she began her probe.

'Where did you go last night, Larry?' she asked abruptly.

He whipped the Mercedes past a Peugeot 504, then stormed up the road with the speedometer needle at 180 k.p.h.

'Last night, ma'am?'

'You are driving too fast!'

'Sorry, ma'am,' and the needle drifted down to 130.

'I asked you where you were last night.'

'In the hotel, ma'am.'

She clenched her hands into fists.

'Don't lie to me!' She was shocked to hear how shrill her voice sounded. She paused, then controlling her voice, she went on, 'I wanted to speak to you. They told me you had gone out. Where did you go?'

He shot the car past a Jaguar. The driver tapped his horn as a protest at the speed of the Mercedes.

'You are driving too fast, Larry . . . stop it!'

'Yes, ma'am,' and the speed of the car slackened.

'Where were you last night?' she persisted.

'I went for a walk.' He glanced at her, then away. 'Does that bother you, ma'am?'

The gentle rebuke was like a slap in the face to her. She

was losing her head about this boy, she told herself. Why shouldn't he go for a walk if he wanted to? Because she had longed for him and still longed for him, she realized she was making a drama out of everything he did.

'No ... it didn't bother me,' she said, steadying her voice. 'I just wondered where you were.'

'I took a look at the town.' His jaws moved rhythmically as he chewed. 'It's not much. I got cold. I was glad to get into bed.'

'Yes.' She had a feeling he was lying but she wasn't sure.

They drove for the next hour in silence and it irritated her that he seemed quite happy to drive and not to have to listen to anything she might say. When they came to the entrance to the Bernadino tunnel and he flicked on his dipped headlights, she remembered the call to Hamburg.

She said, 'The hotel charged me for a call to Hamburg. They said you had made it.'

She was watching him, but his face remained relaxed and he continued to chew.

'That's right, ma'am. I made the call. I wanted news of Ron. Excuse me if I did wrong.'

She drew in a long, slow breath. His constant 'excuse me's' were gnawing at her nerves.

'How is Ron?'

'He's okay, ma'am.'

'Have the police released him?'

His eyes shifted to her and then away.

'Yeah.'

'So what is he doing now?'

Watching him, she had a feeling she had dropped salt on a snail. He retreated into a shell. His blank expression, his gum chewing told her it was a shell she wasn't going to penetrate.

'I don't know, ma'am.'

'Didn't you ask him?'

'I didn't speak to him. I spoke to one of his friends. He just told me Ron was out.'

She shrugged. He didn't want to confide in her ... after all, why should he?

The run through the tunnel took some minutes.

'The road ahead is tricky and dangerous, Larry. I know it well. I will drive,' she said when she saw they were reaching the end of the tunnel.

'Just as you say, ma'am.'

She looked at the gas gauge.

'There's a service station not far from the end of the tunnel. We'll change there.'

'Okay, ma'am.'

Ten kilometres beyond the tunnel they came to the service station and Larry stopped the car by the pumps.

He got out and she slid under the driving wheel as the attendant came out of his shelter.

She told him to fill the tank.

Larry came around and got in the passenger's seat.

'Pay him,' she said. 'It'll be thirty francs.'

'What was that, ma'am?'

At the sound of the startled note in his voice, she looked sharply at him. He immediately shifted his eyes.

'I said . . . pay him thirty francs!' she snapped.

He shifted uneasily.

'Excuse me, ma'am . . . I haven't thirty francs,' he said and she saw his face was now beetroot red.

She lifted her hands, then dropped them on her mink covered lap.

'All right, Larry.' She opened her bag and paid the attendant twenty-seven francs and gave him a franc tip. Then she shifted into gear and drove out on to the broad mountain road. When they were out of sight of the gas station, she drew in against the side of the mountain and stopped the car. She turned off the engine, took out her cigarette case and lit a cigarette.

'I would like to get this straight, Larry,' she said.

He looked furtively at her.

'What was that, ma'am?'

'I want an explanation. I gave you three hundred marks in Bonn. The meal couldn't have been more than twenty marks so you had a balance of around two hundred and eighty. I then gave you fifteen hundred francs to get clothes. You told me you had something over from that. You also told me twice that you do not accept money. Now you

57

can't even find thirty francs ... did you lose what I gave you?'

He rubbed the side of his jaw as he hesitated, then he nodded.

'Yeah ... I guess I did.'

She stared at him.

'But how did you lose all that money, Larry?'

He chewed on his gum and she could see sweat-beads forming on his forehead.

'I guess I just lost it, ma'am.'

'Do you expect me to accept such a stupid answer?' The angry snap in her voice stiffened him. He remained silent, staring through the wind shield at the falling snow.

'It's a lot of money to lose,' she went on, softening her voice when she saw he wasn't going to reply. 'How did you lose it?'

Still he said nothing. If he were wearing his cap she was sure he would be pulling at the peak.

'Larry! Will you please answer my question! Did some woman get it from you last night?'

He moved uneasily, then he nodded.

'I guess that's how it happened, ma'am.'

She thought of the previous evening. The terrible let-down when she had been told he had gone out. She felt so frustrated she couldn't speak for several seconds. Finally she said, her voice unsteady, 'You wanted a woman and you went out in the snow to look for one ... is that right?'

'Yes, ma'am.'

She closed her eyes, her hands turning into fists.

There was a long silence, then she said, 'Tell me about it.'

Again he shifted uneasily.

'There's nothing to tell, ma'am ... excuse me ... I'm sorry.'

'Tell me about it!' Her voice was ugly and harsh.

Startled he looked at her, then away.

'Larry!'

He slumped down in the car seat as if defeated.

'Well, ma'am, if you must know ... I went to a café. There was this girl on her own. We got talking.' He ran his fingers through his hair. 'Maybe you can understand. I wanted her. We went to her place. She had a girl friend there.' He stared through the wind shield, frowning. 'I guess they took me to the cleaners. When I got back to the hotel I hadn't five francs left.'

Two girls! Helga drew in a shuddering breath. You stupid, beautifully built fool! You could have had me for nothing and in comfort!

'You seem to have bad luck with your girls, don't you?' she said and shifted the gear lever into *Drive*.

'You could say that, ma'am. I guess I'm not so hot with women.'

Looking at him, seeing him slumped in depression, she felt a pang of pity for him.

She drove along the mountain road and began the difficult descent towards Bellonzona.

Herman Rolfe liked to spend a month, during the winter, in Switzerland. The snowcapped mountains and the clean blue sky had a fascination for him. He had bought a four-bedroom villa at Castagnola, overlooking the lake of Lugano, had finished it and made use of it during the month of February.

The villa had been built by a successful movie director some fifteen years ago when land and building were at a reasonable price. The villa was rather special as it hung from the mountain side, was screened by eight foot high walls, had two hectares of land and had an unrivalled view of the lake and the tiny villages around the lake. It had a heated swimming pool, a glassed-in patio, a games and movie room, plus all the luxury gimmicks a movie director at the height of his success could dream up. There was also a garage for four cars with staff quarters over the garage.

Each February, Helga came to Switzerland to get the villa ready for her husband's reception.

He would eventually arrive with Hinkle who acted as his nurse, his valet and his chef. Hinkle had been in Rolfe's service for some fifteen years. He looked like a benign English bishop: rotund, bald, with white wisps of hair to soften his florid complexion. He was as smooth as silk in his manner, spoke only when spoken to and was unbelievably efficient in everything he did. Although looking older than his fifty years, he was also athletic and surprisingly strong.

Helga had come to admire him. She quickly realized he tolerated nothing but the best. Anything that was less than best was instantly condemned by him. At first she had been afraid of him. During the first two months of her marriage, she knew he was observing her, judging her and he made her horribly nervous. Then he seemed to accept the fact that she was as efficient in her job as a hostess and as a personal secretary and as a wife as he was in his various jobs. She realized this when flowers began to appear in her bedroom and then other things happened to make her life much easier and she knew this was Hinkle's way of telling her she was accepted. He still remained aloof, but when their eyes met, his expression was benign.

In three days from now, she thought as she drove towards Lugano, her husband and Hinkle would be arriving at the villa. From Bonn she had already alerted the cleaning agency in Lugano to put the villa in order and to turn on the heating. She always stayed at the Eden hotel in Lugano while this was going on. When the villa was ready, she drove to the tiny airport at Agno to meet her husband's private plane and then drive him to the villa.

But now she had Larry with her, she didn't intend to stay at the Eden hotel. The cleaning would be done. The heating would be on. Food was no problem. The deep freeze cabinet was always kept well stocked for an unexpected arrival.

Three days!

To have this boy to herself for three days turned Helga hot. It was a risk. They would arrive at the villa at 14.00. But since Herman and she came only to Castagnola for a month in the year they had no social life nor did they know anyone in the district. It was only a slight risk, she assured herself. There was no one to raise eyebrows or to gossip.

Now was the moment, she thought as she drove down the narrow, twisting road that led directly to the lake, to alert Larry. She would have to handle him gently. He was such an odd mixture. She thought of the two girls. They could have drained him of all sexual desire. He might think a woman older than himself undesirable in his present mood ... she doubted that. A man of his build must have a lot of resilience, but she must be careful.

'Tell me, Larry, what are you plans?' she asked abruptly.

He gave a little start as if startled to find her by his side.

'My plans, ma'am?' He chewed for a long moment. 'I guess I'll look for a job.'

'Do you think you'll get one?'

'Oh, sure ... I've got jobs before. Yeah, I'll get one all right.'

'But you'll need a work permit, Larry.'

He glanced at her, then lifted his heavy shoulders.

'Is that right? Well, I guess I'll have to get a work permit then.'

She restrained her exasperation with an effort.

'I don't think you know really what you are saying,' she said as gently as she could. 'Work permits here are difficult to get. Now listen, Larry, I want to help you. I know you're against accepting money, but I would like to make you a loan. You must have some money while you try to get a work permit. You can always pay me back later.'

He shook his head.

'Thanks, ma'am, but I'll manage. I appreciate the offer. My old man would flip his lid if he knew I was taking money from anyone.'

'But your father won't know unless you tell him,' Helga said as if speaking to a child.

He remained silent for so long she looked sharply at him. He was staring blankly at the car ahead of them, chewing, his face screwed into an expression of thought. She decided not to hurry him and she waited as she drove into the thick traffic and into the centre of Lugano.

Finally, he said, 'Well, ma'am, I appreciate it. You're right about my old man. I needn't tell him, but it bothers me that I might not be able to pay you back. I've cost you enough already.'

'Suppose you let me bother about that?' She was now happy, realizing at last she had broken through the crust of his obstinacy and was reaching him. 'You see, Larry, money

61

doesn't mean a great deal to me. I have it, and when I can help people, it makes me happy to do it.'

He took a little time to consider this, then he nodded.

'Yeah ... I guess I would feel the same way too, ma'am, if I had money.'

They were now driving along the lake at a crawl. The traffic along the lake was always slow and congested.

'It's pretty, isn't it?' she said.

'It sure is, ma'am.' He looked at the lake glittering in sudden pale sunlight and at the distant hills with the snow covering the trees. 'What do they call this place?'

'This is Lugano. We are now going to my home. I'd like you to see it. It's not far from here.'

'Your home?' He turned and looked at her, his jaw moving as he chewed and he smiled his warm smile that set her blood on fire. 'I didn't expect to be taken to your home.'

She laughed.

'Why not? You can stay the night ... there's plenty of room, then I will see what I can do for you tomorrow.'

'You mean you are asking me to stay the night in your home?'

'Why not?'

He slammed his big hands down on his knees with such violence she was sure he had hurt himself.

'Boy!' he exclaimed. 'Am I lucky! Boy! Boy! Am I lucky!'

Helga looked sharply at him. There was just too much exuberance in his voice to ring true. She had a moment of doubt, even fear, but as he swivelled to look at her, his smile so warm and friendly, the doubt and the fear went away.

'I'm glad you're pleased, Larry.'

'You don't know what this means to me, ma'am,' he said. 'I was getting scared. I couldn't see myself sleeping rough in a place like this. I couldn't think where I was going to sleep.'

You'll sleep with me, Helga thought as she said, 'Don't worry about that, Larry.' She smiled at him, resisting the urge to put her hand on his. 'Don't worry about anything.'

Helga lay on the king-size bed, her nakedness covered by

62

her black chiffon wrap, her arms and legs spread wide in total relaxation. She looked around her big bedroom contentedly.

It was a beautiful room with apricot-coloured leather padded walls, mirrors, a wall-to-wall fitted white wool carpet and fume oak fitted furniture. A mirror, facing the vast bed, told her she looked sensually beautiful and fifteen years younger than she was.

She and Larry had stopped in Castagnola at a small restaurant and had the expected greasy Swiss meal of pork chops and chips, then she had driven him up the St. Moritz highway to the villa.

She had been pleased by his reaction to the villa. His stunned expression as she unlocked the heavy oak, nail studded front door and took him through the lobby and into the vast living-room gave her an excited lift until she remembered her own astonishment when she had first walked into the room.

'Gee!' He stood staring around. 'This is really something! It's just out of the movies!'

'It is . . . it was once owned by a movie director. Take your coat off. Look around.'

Together they explored the house. At first, he made exclamations of surprise as the luxury of the place unfolded before him. He gaped at the indoor, heated swimming pool, looked through the double-glazed windows at the outdoor swimming pool and the big terrace and the distant view of Lugano. He began to grow silent as he stood in the movie projection room with its twenty plush seats and the vistavision screen. He just stood, saying nothing as she showed him the four bedrooms, each with their de luxe bathrooms. Then she began to realize that so much luxury and comfort was making a bad impression on him. There were other things to show him: two sauna baths, the tiny elevator that conveyed logs from the cellar right to the big fireplace, the two chair lifts that would take you down to the main highway if you wanted to go for a walk and didn't want to descend the hundred steps through the garden. There was the kitchen with its push button miracles, fully equipped to produce a dinner for twenty people, the stereo radio and gramophone that could produce music in every room or in any room provided you pressed the right button. Also the colour TV set in every room, the deep freeze cabinet, the speaker-boxes hooked to the telephone which allowed you to talk to anyone in any city in the world without moving from your chair: tiny loudspeakers so finely tuned you could hear someone breathing in Tokyo ... so many other things but she saw now that like a child fed too many chocolates, he was turning sour, perhaps even sick at so much luxury.

She broke off the sight-seeing tour and said, 'I'll show you your room. It's just across the way.'

She opened a door and led him through a covered passage to another door. She unlocked it, mounted stairs and into a narrow passage with three doors leading from it. The first door led to Hinkle's room. The next door led to a bathroom. The third door led to a small room which was seldom used. She opened the door.

'Make yourself at home, Larry. Use the bathroom. I want to unpack and change. I'll telephone you in an hour or so. If you want to wander around, go ahead. Be at home.'

He looked into the room, his jaws moving as he chewed.

'I guess you must have a lot of money, ma'am,' he said and she was aware of a sullen note in his voice.

'My husband has ... I haven't.' She smiled. 'We'll have a picnic tonight. There s plenty of food in the deep freeze,' and moving around him, she walked back to the villa.

She had unpacked, taken a bath and then dropped on to the bed.

The time was now 17.45 and it was dark. The San Salvatore mountain with its twin radio and TV masts was obscured by cloud. The lights of Lugano showed dimly through the haze. The amber light in the big bedroom emphasized the apricot coloured walls and was kind to her reflection in the mirror.

Now was the time for love, she thought and her body melted with her desire. She lifted the telephone receiver and pressed button 10 which connected her with Larry's room. There was a long pause and her heart contracted. Surely he was there? Then just when she was getting into a panic, his voice came over the line.

'Yeah, ma'am?'

'Come and see me. Follow the blue lights. They will bring you to me.'

'What was that again, ma'am?'

She moved impatiently, closing her legs tightly together.

'When you leave your room, you will see blue lights in the ceiling, Larry,' she said, controlling the impatience in her voice. 'If you will follow the lights, they will lead you to my room.'

'Sure, ma'am. I'll do that,' and he hung up.

She reached for the battery of buttons built into the side of the bed and pressed the blue button, then she waited. She looked a little anxiously at her reflection in the opposite mirror. Suppose he turned shy? Suppose . . . no! He was a young animal. He had admitted to her he had this sexual urge. Again she looked at the reflection in the mirror and she was satisfied.

She waited, and as she waited, she heard him coming up the stairs. She hoped he wasn't chewing gum. There was a long pause, and then a tap came on the door.

Instinctively she pulled the wrap around her, suddenly worried it might be too transparent.

'Come on in, Larry,' she called, and now she wanted him as she had never wanted any other man before.

He came in.

Could it be possible? she thought as she forced a smile. He was still wearing his dark suit, his white shirt and black tie!

When he saw her lying on the bed, the black chiffon wrap scarcely concealing the whiteness of her body, he stiffened and stepped back.

'Excuse me, ma'am,' he said awkwardly and began to back out of the room.

'Oh, come on in, Larry!' Even to her, her voice sounded waspish. 'Shut the door!'

He shut the door, remaining still, his eyes shifted to her, then shifted away.

'You're not shy of me, are you?' she said, thinking: God! if this flops, I'll kill myself!

'I guess not, ma'am.'

'Come here.'

He moved slowly to the bed, then he stood over her, looking down at her.

'Gee! You're beautiful! I've never seen anyone so beautiful!'

It was a spontaneous outburst that set a flame to her body. She held out her hand. He took it and she pulled him down on the bed.

'You're over dressed, Larry,' and her fingers pulled his tie loose.

'Is it all right, ma'am? You're sure it's all right.'

'For God's sake! You're not a kid, are you?'

Her frantic fingers began to unbutton his shirt.

He pulled away from her.

'I'll do it, ma'am. May I see you . . . may I look at you?'

She opened her wrap, revealing her nakedness.

'Oh, ma'am.'

He was gazing at her as she found the zip of his trousers.

As she pulled, he began to struggle out of his jacket. His hand slipped and banged against the row of buttons which controlled the lights, the TV set and all the other gimmicks in the villa. There came a blinding flash and then complete darkness. She had his fly open. She felt him jerk away from her. She lay still, her heart hammering, her eyes blinded by the flash and the darkness.

'What's happened?' she asked, her voice husky.

'I touched something,' Larry said out of the darkness. 'I guess I've tripped a fuse. I'll fix it. You wait here.'

'To hell with the fuse! Larry!' She lifted herself up and stared into the darkness. 'Larry!'

'I'll fix it.'

From the sound of his voice he was already out of the room and she heard his footfalls as he stumbled down the corridor.

I don't want you to fix it, you goddam, stupid fool! she thought as she lay back on the bed. Who the hell cares about a fuse! Come back! I want you to love me!

She waited a long moment, hearing him blundering about somewhere in the darkness, then she got off the bed. Pulling her wrap around her, she groped her way to the door. She could see nothing in the darkness.

'Larry!'

She heard a door open and then slam shut.

'Come back!' she screamed. 'Larry? Do you hear me?'

She stood in the darkness, listening. The silence and the darkness weighed down on her.

She made the effort and controlled her frustrated anger. God! what a hick this boy was! Somehow he had blown a fuse and he had this stupid inferiority complex that he had to mend it immediately! She groped her way back to the bed. The distant lights on the highway made a small light in the room and she could see the outline of the bed. She sank on to it.

She felt cold and she was shaking. The fool had blown a fuse just when she had been offering herself to him. Yet he had left her to go down to the cellar to mend the fuse! Was she so undesirable? Or was there something wrong about him? Perhaps he was only excited by very young girls. Hot tears rose to her eyes and spilled over. Maybe he wasn't the young, sexual animal she had thought he was.

She waited. Nothing happened and silence brooded over the villa, then she thought of him groping around in the blacked out cellar, trying to mend a fuse. He could kill himself! She remembered there was a flashlight in one of the many drawers built in by her bed. She had to scrabble through three drawers before she found it. She switched it on. Its bright beam was comforting. She searched for and found her pantie briefs and slipped them on, then picking up the flashlight, she went quickly from the bedroom, down the short corridor, past the living-room to the stairs that led to the cellars.

At the head of the stairs, she paused and called, 'Larry!'

Silence greeted her and a wave of cold panic ran over her. The fool couldn't have killed himself? Had he electrocuted himself in the dark? She stood motionless. Suppose he had? Suppose he was lying dead before the fuse boxes? What would she do? How would she explain what he had been doing here to get himself electrocuted?

Cold and shaking, she started down the stairs. Ahead of

her was the door leading to the fuse boxes and the central heating apparatus. She could hear the motor roaring behind the heavy steel door. The door was shut. She hesitated before opening it, then pushed down the steel lever and forced the door open.

'Larry?'

Except for the violent beat of the electric motor, she heard nothing. She hesitated to go further, then bracing herself, she lifted the beam of the flashlight and shakily moved the beam into the big-hot room.

There was no sign of Larry. She moved into the room and played the beam on the fuse boxes. She saw the green button was out and the red button was in. After a moment's hesitation, she pushed the green button home. The light in the boiler room came on. Turning, she moved into the corridor turned on the switch and the three overhead lights in the corridor came on.

Puzzled and frightened, she hurried back up the stairs to her bedroom. The defused light above her bed was now on. She whirled around and ran along the corridor, down the stairs, turning on the switches as she went until she came to the corridor leading underground to the garage and the staff quarters. Holding her wrap around her, she opened the door, turned on the light and hurried along the corridor, up the stairs until she reached the three rooms reserved for the staff. She went to the end room and threw open the door to find the small room empty.

She stood in the doorway, her heart beating violently, looking around. She remembered Larry had left the cheap plastic suitcase by the bed. It had gone. The bed was undisturbed. She turned around, flicked up the light switch and walked to the bathroom and then to Hinkle's room. Both rooms were empty. She paused for a moment, then walked with shaking legs back to her bedroom.

In her bedroom, she paused.

Where was Larry? What had happened to him?

She pressed her cold hand against her forehead as she tried to think. There must be some explanation. He had either panicked and had run away or he had met with an accident while groping around in the dark. He could have

68

fallen in the pool, down some of the many stairs ... anything!

She must get some clothes on! She dressed swiftly and as she slipped on her shoes, she began to feel calmer. There was a fibre of steel in her that always supported her in emergencies and she drew on it now.

Bracing herself, she went through all the rooms in the villa. Then not finding Larry, she returned to her room, put on her mink coat and gloves and went down to the garage.

The Mercedes was where Larry had parked it. She even opened the boot to make certain he wasn't playing some fool practical joke on her. She went to the outdoor swimming pool and shone the beam of the flashlight over the blue water, half expecting to see Larry's submerged body, but only the glittering water met her eyes.

It was bitterly cold and the frosty air nipped at her.

Where was he ... damn him!

She looked with despair at the dark garden spread out below her, now lit by the rising moon. She had to be sure he hadn't stumbled down the steep steps and hurt himself. She had to be sure.

She started down the steps, moving the beam of her flashlight, and every now and then, she stopped and called, 'Larry!' It wasn't until she reached the wrought iron gates that led directly to the St. Moritz highway that she convinced herself he wasn't on the estate.

The fool! The hick! The damn, stupid, juvenile jerk!

Seeing her half naked must have panicked him. This stupid, clumsy act that had fused the lights had been an excuse to run away from her. He was incapable of loving a matured woman. All he wanted was some giggling, stupid, undeveloped teenager! She felt so frustrated and furious that she raised her clenched fists above her head and shook them.

She rode back in the chair lift to the villa.

Back in her bedroom, she stripped off her mink coat and let it drop on the floor. She pressed her hands against her cold face, then she looked in the mirror, opposite the bed. She stiffened. Was this white-faced, gaunt, desperately old looking woman her? Could it be her?

'Damn him to hell!' she said, half aloud, staring at her reflection. 'I must be going out of my mind! A gum-chewing little bastard like that! I've got to stop this! I've got to control myself! If I go on like this, I'll be found out, then my life as I know it, as I like it, will be finished! I've got to stop it and I'm going to stop it!'

Aware she was trembling, she stood motionless, drawing in slow, deep breaths, then when she felt steadier, she left the room and went along to the sitting-room. She stood in the vast room, looking around: its vastness and loneliness crushed her.

She couldn't spend the night here, she told herself. She must have contact with other people. She would call the Eden hotel. They would have a room for her. She would have a lonely, but good dinner in the grill room, then sleeping pills would give her release until the morning but first she had to have a drink.

She crossed to the well stocked bar and poured a heavy slug of vodka into a crystal tumbler. She added ice from the refrigerator and a dash of martini, then she carried the drink to one of the big settees. She sat down, sipped her drink and lit a cigarette.

She stared through the picture window at the distant view, the haze and the lights. She refused to let herself think until she had finished the drink, then getting up, she made another and then returned to the settee.

She was now calmer and her shrewd mind began to regain its keenness. She was suddenly appalled at the risk she had taken. To bring an unknown boy to her home as she had done had been utter lunacy! Her sex urge must be stamped out! She drew in a long shuddering breath. Well, he was gone! Thank God he had been a hick, and thank God the sight of her nakedness had frightened him away!

She stubbed out her cigarette and immediately lit another.

Never again!

If she had to have a man she must look for an hotel servant in an hotel in which she wasn't known ... something like that.

But at the back of her mind there was a growing feeling of

70

uneasiness. The gum-chewing boy had taken a lot of money from her. The passport alone had cost three thousand francs. Might he not come back for more? Might he not consider her an ideal subject for blackmail?

Helga had been trained in law, had worked with ruthless business men and she was well aware of the dangers of blackmail.

She felt her hands turn moist as she sat, thinking.

But after a little thought, stamping down on her panic, she began to relax. No, he wouldn't dare blackmail her. He couldn't! She knew his passport was faked. Of course she had more to lose than he, but in a showdown, she had a weapon she could and would use.

She finished her drink.

Fortified now by two cocktails, she felt much more relaxed. She remembered his warm, friendly smile. A boy who could smile like that couldn't be a blackmailer nor could he have anything bad in him. Then she remembered his quiet words to that little pansy: *What would it cost you if you got your hands crushed in a door?* She felt a chill run up her spine. But he was bluffing, she assured herself. He had told her he fed on the violence of television. That had been the threat of a small boy . . . no, it was all right: he was a hick, and that was that. She could put him out of her mind.

It had been a moment of madness . . . now she must forget it.

She went across the room and telephoned the Eden hotel.

The Reception manager's welcome flattered, soothed and pleased her.

'Yes, of course, Madame Rolfe. I have your usual suite. Only too delighted. And how is Mr. Rolfe?'

She said her husband was fairly well, that she would be arriving in about half an hour and would he reserve a table for her in the grill room?

She hung up and went to her bedroom. Taking a small suitcase from one of the many closets, she packed what she would need for the night. As she was closing the lid of the suitcase, she paused and stiffened.

Had she heard something? She listened again, hearing

only the beating of her heart. Moving silently, she went to the bedroom door and opened it. She stood in the open doorway, looking along the lighted corridor, tense, her ears straining. She now could only hear the muffled roar of the motor, driving the central heating and then the slight whirr from the deep freeze cabinet in the kitchen. She frowned, annoyed with herself for imagining odd sounds, then as she was about to turn back to her room, she again paused and stiffened.

She was sure now she had heard a sound. A footfall? A door shutting? A door opening? Some sound that didn't blend in with the expected sounds of the villa.

She listened but could hear nothing now.

Had Larry come back?

She moved into the corridor, her heart thumping, her breathing a little laboured. She waited, listening, then she heard the sound again: a door closing softly. There could be no mistaking that sound. All the doors in the villa were of heavy oak. It was impossible to close them silently. Every one of them gave out a little clicking sound no matter how carefully they were shut.

There was someone in the villa!

Was it Larry?

Panic surged through her until she got hold of herself. She turned swiftly back into her bedroom, ran across to one of the closets, opened the door, slid open a drawer and her hand dropped on a .22 automatic pistol: a tiny, but vicious weapon she had often carried in the streets of New York when a woman with her looks had to have protection after dark. The gun gave her a feeling of security, and with this feeling of security, she began also to feel angry.

She went to the open door of the bedroom.

'Who's there?' she called, pitching her voice high.

Silence greeted her. She hesitated only for a moment, then lifting the gun, she aimed it at the door at the far end of the corridor and squeezed the trigger.

The bang of the gun sounded very loud in the stillness of the villa. A tiny hole appeared in the woodwork of the door and splinters flew.

At least, she thought, whoever it was in the villa now

knew she had a gun. Bracing herself, she went down the corridor and threw the door open. There was nothing to see: only the lights, the thick royal blue carpet and the corridor leading to the front door. Again she paused to listen, but although she remained motionless for several nerve-racking minutes, she heard nothing to alarm her further.

Still holding the gun, she went back to the bedroom. She put on her coat, her hat and gloves. She was fighting off a growing panic as she paused to look at her pale, drawn face in the mirror. Then holding the gun in her right hand and the suitcase in her left hand, leaving all the lights on, she walked warily down the corridor, opened the front door, hesitated for a moment, then switched on the lights to the garage. She put down her suitcase and locked the front door. Turning, she walked swiftly to the security of the Mercedes.

CHAPTER FOUR

In her luxury suite at the Eden hotel, Helga had just finished dressing for dinner when the telephone bell buzzed.

She looked at the telephone for a brief moment, frowning. She wasn't expecting any calls. With Larry still on her mind, anything unexpected made her uneasy. As the buzzer sounded again, she crossed the room and picked up the receiver.

'Is that you, Helga?'

Her eyebrows lifted. She would know that booming voice anywhere. There was a time when Jack Archer went in for amateur theatricals. He had often said that only two men in the world had real actor's voices: Sir Laurence Olivier and himself.

'Why, Jack ... this is a surprise. I've only been here an hour.'

'How are you? Did you have a good run from Bonn?'

'Not bad ... a lot of snow. Where are you, Jack?'

'I've just blown in. I'm in the bar.'

'You mean you're in the hotel?'

'That's it. I flew in from Lausanne yesterday. You said you would be arriving today ... remember?'

She now did remember she had written to him from Paradise City giving the date of her arrival, but she had forgotten. She stiffened, thinking what an escape she had had. Suppose he had come to the villa in search of her and had walked in when she and Larry were there!

'I was planning to drive over to Lausanne tomorrow and see you,' she said, forcing her voice to sound casual.

'I have other business here, Helga, so I thought I'd save you the trip. Are you alone?'

'Of course.'

'Well, how about dinner together?'

'Yes . . . lovely.' She looked at her watch, noticing her hand was a little unsteady. The time was 20.35. 'I'll come right down.'

'In the bar.'

She hung up and stood motionless for some moments. Every six months she went to Lausanne and she and Archer checked through Rolfe's investments. Their intimacy had died abruptly on the day Helga had married. Neither of them ever referred to it. They had now an easy friendship and a good business relationship. Archer had a flair for investment. Sometimes he was a little reckless, and it was then that Helga put the brakes on, but this seldom happened, and when she refused one of his more reckless suggestions, he would grin at her, shrug and say, 'Well, eventually it'll be your money. If you don't want to speculate that's okay with me.'

She found him sitting at a corner table, away from the sprinkling of people in the bar. He stood up and waved to her as she came in.

She thought a little sadly that age never helps anyone. Five year ago, Archer had been one of the handsomest men she had seen off the movies. Now his straw-coloured hair was thinning and receding. He had put on too much weight. Standing over six feet, powerfully and heavily built, he still made an impressive figure, but she could no longer call him handsome. He must be five years older than herself, she thought as she smiled at him, taking his hand.

He had already ordered her a double vodka martini, knowing her drink, and he began asking her questions about her trip as he led her to the table.

She felt relaxed in his company. He had a soothing manner and a lot of charm: one of his major assets when dealing with the very rich. She skirted around her journey, not mentioning she had stayed at the Adlon hotel in Basle. She told him about the new car.

'And what news of Herman?'

She lifted her shoulders.

'The same . . . always busy.'

75

He looked at her thoughtfully, his bright blue eyes a little probing.

'No regrets, Helga?'

'Don't let's go into that.' She finished her drink. She was not going to remember that it had been Archer who had arranged the marriage. She had put enough business his way to reward him. She was certainly not lifting the curtain on those exciting moments in his office when he used to lock the door and they had had those 'quickies' on the settee. 'Let's eat . . . I'm starving.'

The dinner of finely cut smoked beef with pickled cucumbers followed by a pheasant was impeccable.

While waiting for the dessert trolley, she said, 'I didn't know you had other clients in Lugano, Jack.'

'A couple of old fossils.' He grinned. 'I have to see them about every eighteen months. I thought it would be a good idea – save you the trip too – if I came over and did our business and theirs at the same time. Feel like working after dinner?'

She nodded. She had nothing else to do but to worry and brood so she welcomed having him for the rest of the evening.

'I have all the papers in my suite,' he went on. 'Let's go up after coffee . . . okay?'

She hesitated. Was it wise to go to his room? Would eyebrows be raised? He saw her hesitation and immediately read her thoughts.

'They have a small boardroom here. Let's use that,' he said. 'The table will make it easier to spread the papers on.'

She smiled at him, nodding. That was another thing she liked about Archer. He was highly perceptive, tactful and always had a solution.

After the dessert, he said, 'Meet me in the lobby in five minutes. We can have our coffee in the boardroom.'

Half an hour later, the table strewn with papers, the coffee pot empty, Archer paused to light a cigar.

'That about wraps it up, Helga,' he said. 'Not a very good six months, but these Euro-dollar bonds are sliding. Nothing to worry about. They'll come back. At least, they pay a hefty interest. The equities are down ... but the Dow Jones has been shot to hell. Still, it could be worse. Would you like me to explain about the losses to Herman or will you do it?'

'I'll do it. He can't expect to win all the time. I'd like to look at the prices to compare them with last month's figures. How much are we down, Jack?'

He regarded the glowing end of his cigar and lifted his heavy shoulders.

'A damn sight less than most investors.'

She regarded him.

'I'm not in the least interested in other investors, Jack. How much are we down?'

'Oh ... around ten per cent. It'll pick up on the next half year.'

'Ten per cent!' She sat upright. 'But that's about a two million dollar loss!'

'Yes ... about that, but there's twenty million in the kitty.' He smiled. 'My two old fossils are in the hole for a thousand.' He shook his head. 'In comparison, they are worse off than Herman ... a lot worse off.'

'Let me see the stock list.'

He shrugged, opened his briefcase and took out a file.

'Sure you want to run through all this? Could take couple of hours.' He glanced at his watch. 'You must be tired.'

'I'm all right.' She took the file from him and put it on the table.

'To save time, you might initial each page as you go. I've initialled my copy already.' He handed her a gold Parker pen and then began to gather up the papers strewn on the table.

Helga lit a cigarette, picked up the pen and began to go through the list of holdings. She had an excellent memory but there was such a mass of holdings she couldn't remember the exact price of each stock or bond as it had stood six months ago, but she remembered a number of them.

Admittedly the prices of the bonds were down, but only by two or three points. She had been expecting something much more dramatic. She turned the pages, her eyes darting down the neatly typed columns of prices.

Archer sat in an easy chair, watching her, his cigar burning evenly.

'There's a page missing, Jack,' she said finally.

'No . . . you have it all there.'

She looked up sharply.

'There's a page missing. There are at least four Euro-bonds not listed: Mobile, Transalpine, National Financial, Chevron. There are equities missing too. Calcomp. Hobart.' She paused to look at the list, then went on, 'CBS.'

He smiled.

'What a wonderful memory you have. It's really remarkable. Yes, they are missing. You slipped up on one: General Motors.'

She put down the stock list.

'Then let me have the missing page . . . what is this: a memory test?'

'Do you think Herman would miss them from the list?'

She frowned, staring at him.

'Why, no. You know he never looks at all this. You check it . . . I check it . . . and that's it.' She looked more closely at him. 'What is all this about, Jack?'

'Have you initialled the sheets?'

'No, and I'm not going to until I get the missing page.'

He stared at his cigar for a long moment, frowning slightly, then he looked up, staring at her, his pale blue eyes hard.

'You're not getting that, darling.'

She leaned back in her chair.

'Why not?'

'Because they don't exist any more.'

She felt suddenly cold and a little sick. She had been in the jungle of finance long enough to sense what he was trying to tell her.

'All right, Jack . . . explain.'

'One of those things, I'm afraid,' he said and lifted his shoulders. 'That Australian nickel thing . . . I went into it heavily . . . the bubble burst . . . and that's it.'

'*You* went into it heavily . . . what do you mean?'

He made an impatient movement which he checked immediately.

'Oh, come on, Helga! There was a great chance ... a chance of a lifetime! I got in on the ground floor at $10 ... imagine! I held on too long ... it happens. I could have got out at $120, but I just couldn't resist hanging on. I swore I'd get out at $150 and I would have done. Then they found there was no nickel and ... that was that.'

'But where did the money come from?'

'Where do you think? I sold these missing bonds and stocks. Now look, Helga, Herman needn't know about this. You know he never checks anything. He's far too busy. You initial all this stuff and he accepts it. I'm asking you to help me out of a hole. After all he's worth around sixty million ... he'll never miss two, will he?'

'*You* sold bonds and stocks?' Helga sat forward and stared at him. 'But you couldn't have! We have joint signatures on the account! What are you talking about?'

Again he regarded the burning end of his cigar, then he looked at her, then away.

'I always did say, Helga, you had rather an unformed signature.'

She couldn't believe what she was hearing.

'Are you drunk?'

'I wouldn't mind being drunk.' He smiled his charming, sincere smile. 'I'm sorry ... I admit it's a mess, but messes do happen.'

'Are you telling me you forged my signature?'

He hesitated and for a moment, his heavy face darkened.

'Sounds hellish, doesn't it? But that's what I did.'

'You must be out of your mind!'

He lifted his hands.

'I suppose I was then, but it looked so certain. I could have cleaned up three million.'

She put her hands to her eyes. She couldn't bear to look at him. There was a long, heavy silence, then he broke it by saying, 'I'm sorry. It seemed so certain.'

She snatched her hand away and her eyes snapped as she said furiously. 'All weak, stupid, greedy, dishonest fools say that! Don't give me that crap! You've broken a trust! Worse ... you've proved yourself a thief and a forger!'

79

He flinched.

'Yes . . . I deserve that.'

'How could you, Jack! How could you have done such a thing?'

He stubbed out his cigar.

'A mad moment . . . don't you have mad moments?'

She felt her heart skip a beat.

'We're not talking about me. We're talking about you.'

'Yes . . . what are you going to do?'

'What is there to do? I must tell Herman. There is nothing else I can do. I won't be party to this. You have done it and you must take the consequences. I'll try to persuade Herman to accept what has happened . . . I'll do that.'

'Herman is an unforgiving, ruthless sonofabitch,' Archer said quietly. 'He's sure to prosecute. Look, Helga, for old times' sake, won't you give me a hand? After all we were lovers . . . I did fix your marriage . . . don't you feel you owe me something?'

'No, and you know it! You wanted me married to Herman to be sure of his account!'

'Just try leaning over backwards a little. Look, suppose you tell him I suggested investing in Australian nickel. You agreed. The stock began to rise so we plunged two million into it. Suppose you tell him we were gambling on his behalf. Do you think he would buy that?'

She hesitated. She realized she couldn't send this man to prison: even now the memory of those 'quickies' was too strong. Yes, she thought she could convince Herman this had been a bad speculation that hadn't come off. She would be contrite and promise him it would never happen again. He was certain to give her a tongue lashing but if she ate enough humble pie he would still leave her in control of his affairs, but only if she got rid of Archer. She would have to do that. From now on she would have to deal with some firm like Spencer, Grove & Manly, stuffy people, but highly respectable and their integrity unquestionable. She could no longer work with Archer. She could no longer trust him.

She lit a cigarette in the effort to steady her nerves.

'All right, I'll persuade Herman to buy it,' she said quietly.

'But I am going to tell him to move the account to Spencer, Grove & Manly. I can't work with you in the future. You understand that?'

'You really think Herman will buy it?' Archer sat forward, relief on his face.

'I said so, didn't I?'

'Then why close the account, Helga? There's no need to. If you're sure he'll buy it we are back on square A.'

She regarded him as if he were a stranger.

'As soon as Herman arrives I will have a letter for him to sign asking you to transfer all his holdings and files to Spencer, Grove & Manly.' She picked up the list of securities and got to her feet. 'I don't ever want to see you again,' and she walked to the door.

'Helga.'

She paused and turned. He was lighting another cigar.

'Well?'

'Is that your last word?'

'Yes,' and she reached for the door handle.

'Don't run away,' he said, a bite in his voice. 'We still have things to talk about.' He paused, staring at her. 'How did you find Larry? He's quite a character, isn't he?'

The Dean of the School of Law where Helga had taken her doctorate had said among many other things that there was a time to bluff and a time to be intelligent enough to know when not to bluff.

Helga had accepted this wisdom during her Law years. When she had bluffed, she had bluffed with a finesse of an expert poker player but when the situation was such she always accepted the inevitable.

The fibre of steel in her would not allow Archer to see the shock his words had on her. Her face expressionless, she turned around, came away from the door and sat down.

'What else is there to talk about?' and even she was surprised how steady her voice sounded.

He regarded her and genuine admiration showed in his eyes.

'I always thought you had guts, Helga, and now I know it for sure. You took that sucker punch like a champion.'

'What else is there to talk about?' she repeated wood-enly.

'Me and you.' He leaned back in the armchair and drew on his cigar. 'You see, Helga, I can't let the account get away from me. You don't imagine I would forge your signature and take all that money from Herman unless I was in a desperate fix? I've not only lost Herman's money, but I have lost my own. Things are bad at the office. The fact is so many of the old fossils have died recently, so many accounts have come to a grinding halt since the new U.S. tax laws that we're scarcely ticking over. Herman's account is about the one thing that keeps us solvent.'

'You should have thought of that before you turned thief and forger,' Helga said harshly.

'I had no alternative. I was in too deep. It was either sink or swim . . . I'm not the sinking type.'

'That I can believe.'

'The fact is I don't intend to lose the account. You and I are going to continue in partnership, and I'll tell you for why. We are both cheats: I am a thief and forger and you are a whore. Neither of us would get any mercy from Herman. If he found us out, we wouldn't survive. You would lose sixty million dollars and I'd go to jail. That's why we are going to remain partners.'

She sat very still.

'What are you threatening me with?' she asked.

He studied her, then nodded his approval. He reached for his briefcase, opened it and took out an envelope.

'This,' he said and flicked the envelope on to the table. It skidded across and landed in her lap.

Her hands, still steady, took the envelope and lifted the flap. She drew out a glossy photographic print that was still a little damp. She studied it, keeping her expression under control although she felt as if ice water was running down her back.

In the photograph, she was lying on her bed, naked and exposed, her hand on Larry's trouser zip, while he appeared to be tearing off his jacket. In spite of her control, she felt the blood draining out of her face. She returned the print to the envelope and put the envelope on the table.

'Thief, forger ... and now blackmailer,' she said unsteadily. 'At last, I'm getting to know you.'

He smiled: a thin smile, but a smile.

'I've already called myself all those names, Helga. I have now got beyond shame. I'm just not going to sink, and I have persuaded myself the end justifies any means. After all, you yourself are no saint, are you?'

'How did you get this photograph?'

'Do you really want to know?' He sank lower in his chair. 'It was a long term operation and a technical achievement. A week ago I went to the villa ... you remember I have a key ... and I concealed a camera in one of the window recesses. The camera was focused on the bed. I had an electrician with me. He worked on the sun lamp switch by the bed. Larry had only to touch the switch to set off the camera shutter, the flash light and trip the fuses. It was quite a performance.'

She drew in a long, slow breath, trying to control her rising fury.

'You mean you hired an electrician to make this blackmail trap?'

He lifted his hands.

'My dear girl, you don't imagine I'm clever enough to do a job like that? But don't worry. He was very well paid. He just thought I was eccentric ... you know the Swiss.'

'And you got someone to process the photograph?'

'Now, come, Helga, I'm not stupid. I hired a dark room of a local photographic store. I did the processing myself. I'm rather good with a camera.'

She sat for a long moment absorbing what he had told her, then she said, 'And Larry?'

'He's quite a character, isn't he?' Archer drew on his cigar and stared up at the ceiling. 'I knew for certain I would have trouble with you. When the money went down the drain, I knew I had to find a means of controlling your first impulse to rush to Herman and tell him what had happened. I also knew Herman would prosecute. Everyone has a weakness that can be exploited in one way or another. We have known each other now for some ten years. I know your weakness.' He looked at her. 'You have been married to an impotent cripple for four years . . . a little more. You will inherit sixty million dollars so long as you behave yourself but I was certain you weren't living like a nun. I decided to bait a hook for you. Frankly, Helga, with any other woman I wouldn't have attempted it: the trouble, the money spent, the rushing here and there would have been too long odds, but with you, I felt it was worth a try. I knew you were arriving in Hamburg to pick up the car. Two days before you arrived I flew to Hamburg and began to look around. I wanted to find a virile, presentable young man without scruples. Not an impossible task in Hamburg where the dregs of the world come together. I found Larry. In the Reeperbahn, if you look hard enough, you are certain to find someone to do anything no matter how disreputable so long as the money is right.' He paused, then went on. 'Larry was trying to persuade a young whore to take him home for nothing. She slapped his face and spat at him. I followed him into the street and we got talking. He asked me for money. He has beguiling warmth, hasn't he? I am a man and you are a woman. I saw through this hick act of his whereas you fell for it as I was sure you would. I told him I had a job for him. We went to a bar and I told him I wanted him to seduce an attractive woman so I could blackmail her. I offered him one thousand dollars to do the job. I felt quite safe telling him this. I was unknown to him: a man who had picked him up in the street. If he refused, then I could walk out and leave him, but, of course, he didn't refuse.' He leaned forward to tap his ash into the ashtray. 'I wasn't sure where you would stay the night in Hamburg, but I knew you were seeing Schultz on business in Bonn and I knew where you always stayed there. I hired a car and drove Larry to Bonn. The more I talked with him, the more I was convinced that you would fall for him; but I wasn't absolutely certain, and I had to be certain. So as a second line of attack, I dreamed up this passport gimmick. In any case, Larry had to have a new passport. He had deserted from the Army and had got mixed up in some riot. The German police and the U.S. Army police were hunting for him. I felt, if played on your generosity, you would fix him up. It was all a gamble, of course, but I knew you well enough to make the odds acceptable. Before I left Bonn I bugged your car. There is a new electronic eavesdropper on the market now that is fantastically efficient. The bug is the size of a thimble and has an impressive range. I then pointed you out to Larry as you arrived at the Königshof hotel. Once I knew Larry had made contact with you and when he told me you wanted to take him to Switzerland, I knew you had swallowed the bait. It remained to be seen if the hook caught hold. I knew your hour of departure and I went on ahead. I was about a half a kilometre ahead of you all the time and I overheard your conversation. I speeded up and called on Friedlander who Larry had told me about. It was easy to bribe him. He promised that his assistant would take photographs of you and Larry when you arrived at his apartment. I have a good photograph of you passing Friedlander three thousand francs. Herman might well ask you why you paid such a sum unless the boy involved, was your lover. Not a strong card, but something. I really pinned my hopes on you taking Larry to the villa. I was driving ahead of you when you left Basle and I heard you telling Larry you wanted him to see your home. I knew my gamble had come off.' He smiled. 'Larry nearly broke my ear drums with his whoop of triumph. He had assured me you would take him to your home and I had betted him another five hundred dollars he wouldn't pull it off.'

Helga stubbed out her cigarette and lit another. She remembered Larry's exuberant cry: 'Boy! Am I lucky! Boy! Boy! Boy!' She remembered she had wondered about that: so this was the explanation.

'Of course it was still a gamble,' Archer went on. 'You could have raped him in the sitting-room, but I know your style. When there is a bed handy, you use a bed. Anyway, I have a photograph and so we are partners.'

'You certainly value your skin, don't you?' she said.

'I told you: I'm not the sinking type. Well, Helga, you now know the situation. Are you running to Herman?'

'I get nothing in return?'

'If you mean you don't get the negatives . . . you don't. But you can forget them. They'll be completely safe. After all, Helga, if you fall, I fall too: we're partners for as long as Herman lives.'

'Where are the negatives?'

He smiled.

'Winging their way safely to my bank in an envelope marked to be opened only in the event of my death. You are a dangerous woman, Helga. I'm taking no chances. I don't say you would try to murder me, but I don't want you to have the slightest temptation to do so. I must admit you nearly gave me a heart attack when you let off that gun.'

Her eyes narrowed. 'So it was you I heard?'

'That's right. While you were hunting for Larry I was getting the camera. You very nearly caught me at it. Incidentally, you had better get an electrician to re-fix the sun ray lamp if you intend to use it.'

'So the negatives will be lodged in your bank,' Helga said. 'The envelope is to be opened in the event of your death. If you die what do you imagine the manager of the bank will do when he sees the contents?' She was probing for information and she regarded him with a contemptuous smile. 'He will destroy the photographs.'

'No, he won't. When he opens the envelope he will find inside another sealed envelope with instructions to send this envelope to Herman. I don't trust you, Helga. I repeat you are a dangerous woman.'

'You're not being fair to me, are you? You live too well. You have become fat and soft. You could drop dead: men of your age are continually dropping dead through over-indulgence. You fly a lot in these little planes. They are not oversafe. You could be killed in a crash. You could have a motoring accident. You could cease to live any time from tonight. You are striking a hard bargain.'

'Put like that I suppose I am, but I would rather be safe than murdered, Helga. You must hope that I keep alive.' He looked at his watch. 'I have a busy day tomorrow. It's my bedtime. Will you please initial the stock list?'

'When are you leaving?'

'Sometime tomorrow afternoon . . . why the interest?'

'I want to think about all this,' she said and got to her feet. 'I'll give you my decision at three o'clock tomorrow afternoon.'

He sat upright and his heavy face became set. For the first

86

time since she had known him she saw him without his smooth charm.

'Decision?' There was a harsh note in his voice she had never heard before. 'What do you mean? You have no choice! I have you where I want you! Initial those pages at once!'

Her lips moved into a stiff smile.

'I agree, Jack ... *you* have me where you want me, but I too have you where *I* want you. I am facing the loss of sixty million dollars: you are facing at least ten years in a Swiss prison. From what I hear the Establissement de l'Orbe isn't a convalescent home.'

His eyes turned vicious.

'You are in no position to threaten me! I know what money means to you! Now, cut this out! Initial those pages!'

She shook her head.

'I have a decision to make. I have to convince myself that all that money is worth being landed with a partner who is a thief, a forger and a blackmailer. I'm not convinced. If I give up sixty million dollars, I will still have my freedom, but you won't. You'll be in jail ... and God! how you will hate that.' She picked up the stock list. 'I'll let you know my decision at three o'clock tomorrow. Give me a telephone call at the villa,' and she went out of the room.

Back in her bedroom, Helga walked over to the window and drew back the drapes. She stood for several minutes looking at the lights of Cassarate, the red sign that spelt out B-R-E, the outline of the mountain and the headlights of the cars coming down from Castagnola. Snow was beginning to fall: something unusual in Lugano. The lake, glittering in the moonlight, looked like a black mirror.

She was surprised at her calmness and how evenly her heart was beating. She had absorbed the shock. She had been manoeuvred into a trap, and now, she had to consider what she was to do.

Turning away from the window, she undressed and put on pale blue pyjamas. With a pack of cigarettes and her lighter in her hand, she got into bed. She settled herself, turned on the reading light and the room lights off. She lit a cigarette, then relaxed. It was in bed with a cigarette that she always did her best thinking.

First, she asked herself how important was it to her to remain the wife of one of the richest men in the world? To make a comparison, she thought back and considered how she had lived while acting as her father's personal assistant and then later, as Archer's. She had earned reasonable money; she had had a lot of fun, freedom and sex. Against this, she had lived in a tiny, rather dreary apartment. She had always had snatched meals and no car of her own. She liked clothes but could never afford the clothes she wanted. When on vacation she had to stay at the less grand hotels and she remembered envying those who could afford the best hotels. She had to queue for a cinema or a theatre seat, not being able to afford the best seats. She ate at a good restaurant only when dated. She never had any jewellery until she married and she liked top class jewellery: especially diamonds. She didn't know until she married the joys of skiing, of tearing through the water in her own high speed motorboat nor owning a Mercedes 300SEL. She thought of her various homes and the servants who gave her constant attention. She thought of the flattering V.I.P. treatment she received at the airports, hotels and luxury restaurants of the world as soon as the name of Rolfe was mentioned.

She finally came to the conclusion that she must cling to her position even if it meant accepting Archer as a partner.

But did she have to accept him?

I would rather be safe than murdered, he had said.

She shook her head.

No! This was stupid and untidy thinking. She knew she could never take a life: even the life of a creature like Archer.

So what was the solution . . . if any?

She thought about this for some time. For her, she finally decided, the ideal solution would be if her husband dropped dead. Men of his age – he must be nearly seventy – were always dropping dead. What a marvellous and fantastic solution to her problem it would be if the telephone bell rang at

88

this moment and Hinkle broke the news to her that Herman had suffered a heart attack. By dying, Herman would free her from this blackmail threat. She would automatically inherit the estate: no doubt, he would leave his daughter something, but if he didn't, she could afford to be generous with all that money. But that wasn't the real magic of Herman's death. The magic of his death would mean she would have Archer in her power as he now had her in his power. She imagined letting him wait until three o'clock the following day. then she would ask him to come to the villa. 'Something I want to discuss with you, Jack,' she would say. 'No, not over an open line. Besides, you want the stock sheets, don't you?' He would come, cautiously perhaps, but triumphant, knowing she had surrendered. She would play with him as a cat plays with a mouse until it would dawn on him he was not going to get the stock list. Then she would listen to his threats and bluster and she would laugh at him.

She paused in her thinking, her eyes narrowing.

I would rather be safe than murdered.

Archer had said that and Archer was also dangerous.

No, before she had her showdown with him, she would have to alert Spencer, Grove & Manly. She had already met Edwin Grove, a tall, dried up looking man at a cocktail party in Lausanne. She would telephone him before Archer arrived, telling him the facts and asking him to take all the necessary action; that Archer would be at her villa in two or three hours, and would he alert the police?

Then when she had finished her tongue-lashing, the police would arrive and take him away.

All this . . . but only if Herman dropped dead.

She stubbed out her cigarette and stared up at the ceiling. She knew instrictively that Herman was going to live for at least another ten years. He had a daily visit from his doctor. He took the greatest care of himself. She remembered the doctor telling her that Herman had a heart of a young man.

She moved restlessly under the sheet.

Dreams!

She forced her mind to become realistic. She was trapped and she might as well admit it. At any rate she would make that fat swine sweat until three o'clock tomorrow, then she would tell him to come to the villa and she would hand him the initialled stock list.

She had been asking for trouble these past four years and now it had arrived. Accept the inevitable, the Dean of the School of Law had once said in one of his dry lectures.

She would have to do that, but that wouldn't stop her hating Archer and hoping something horrible would happen to him . . . but he mustn't die.

She reached for her sleeping pills, took three of them, swallowing them without water with practised ease, then with a little shiver of self-disgust, she reached up and turned off the light.

At 10.00 the following morning, Helga telephoned down to the concierge's desk.

'Is Mr. Archer still in the hotel?'

'No, madame: he left about twenty minutes ago.'

'Thank you . . . it's not important.'

She felt sure Archer would have gone out by now, but she wanted to check. She couldn't have borne running into him in the lobby to see his smirking, fat face and his questioning eyes.

She slipped on her mink coat, glanced in the mirror, adjusted her hat, then picking up the briefcase holding the stock list, she left her suite.

She had the stock lists for the previous month at the villa and she wanted to check the prices against the prices Archer had given her. She wanted to be certain just how much money he had stolen. He had said glibly two million dollars, but she wanted to know the exact sum.

The doorman opened her car door with a flourish. She nodded to him, started the engine, then joined the traffic crawl along the lake.

Drugged by the pills, she had slept heavily and she still felt heavy headed and irritable. The day after tomorrow, she thought, she would have to drive to Agno to meet Herman's plane. She wondered in what mood she would find him. Usually, after a plane trip, he was testy and difficult. She would have to get something out of the deep freeze ready for

Hinkle to cook. Herman was faddy about his food. One of his favourite dishes was breaded veal with spaghetti: this Helga never ate. She had the middle-aged woman's horror of getting fat. There would be filets of veal in the freezer. She would get them out tomorrow.

She stopped at the Migros store at Cassarate and bought onions, a tin of peeled tomatoes and a tin of tomato purée. She knew there would be packets of spaghetti in the store cupboard. She bought a dozen eggs and a litre of milk. Hinkle was a genius at making an omelette which she could always eat. She paused for a moment thinking, but could think of nothing else to buy. With her purchases in a paper bag, she got into the car and drove up the twisting road to Castagnola. She stopped at the Post Office and collected some dozen letters. The girl behind the counter gave her a friendly smile.

'Will you be staying long, madame?'

'Till the end of the month. Please have the letters delivered tomorrow.'

She drove up to the villa. The snow plough had been at work and the road was clear but there were high banks of snow either side of the road and once when she pressed too hard on the gas pedal, the back wheels of the car slipped, a slip she quickly corrected. The private drive to the villa had also been cleared and the roadman had put down grit. The fifty francs she gave him each February was an investment that produced dividends when snow and ice made the drive difficult.

The garage doors, controlled by an electronic beam swung up and she drove in, parking beside Hinkle's 1500 Volkswagen. Collecting the mail, her briefcase and the paper bag, she walked along the underground passage to the villa. She remembered she had left the door from the cellar to the villa unlocked and she frowned at her carelessness. Shrugging, she opened the door, shut and locked it, then walked up the stairs and into the big entrance hall. She put the mail on the table and took off her coat and hat which she left in a recess. She carried her purchases to the kitchen, then she looked at her watch. The time was now 11.15. Time for a drink, she told herself, then she must get down to work. It

CHAPTER FIVE

For a long moment, she stood staring at this big, blond boy aware only of the faint sound of the central heating motor below and the violent beating of her heart.

During that moment, her mind was paralysed by shock, then her resilience absorbed the shock and fury gripped her, sending blood to her face, making the veins in her neck throb and giving her face an expression of vicious rage.

'How dare you come back!' she screamed at him. 'Get out! Do you hear me! Get out!'

He flinched, then rubbed the side of his mouth with the back of his hand.

'Excuse me, ma'am . . . I had to see you.'

She strode to the door and threw it open.

'Get out or I'll call the police!'

The moment she had said it, she knew she had lost control of herself. Police? The last thing she would want was a curious Swiss policeman here. She forced down her rage and her mind began to function. What was he doing here . . . more blackmail! He wouldn't dare! He was an Army deserter . . . and yet Archer was a thief and a forger and he hadn't hesitated to blackmail her. Could this lout of a boy realize what she stood to lose if he gave her away?

But she was determined to intimidate him.

'Get out!' she screamed at him.

'Ma'am . . . please . . . won't you listen to me? I want to say I'm sorry.' He twisted his cap, his face in despair. 'Honestly, ma'am . . . I want you to believe me . . I'm sorry.'

She drew in a deep breath, controlling her fury.

'Rather late, isn't it?' she said bitterly. 'Sorry? After what you have done? After the way I treated you? You have the impudence to come here and tell me you're sorry. Oh, go away! The sight of you sickens me!'

'Yeah ... I guess you have reason.' He shuffled his feet. 'Ma'am, I want to help you. When I told Ron, he said I was a dirty sonofabitch. He said if I didn't do something about this, he'd never speak to me again.'

Helga stiffened.

'You told Ron?'

'Yes, ma'am. I told him last night on the phone. You see, ma'am, I owe him money. This fat guy gave me fifteen hundred dollars. I guess I was a little excited. I haven't had so much money in one lump before. I told Ron I was buying a second-hand car and then he wanted to know how I got the money ... so I told him.'

How many more were going to know what a reckless, mad fool she had been? she thought. This boy, that awful little queer, Archer and now this man, Ron.

She went over to the bar, poured a large slug of vodka into a glass and without bothering to add ice, she gulped it down. The neat spirit made her eyes water, but it knitted her together so she ceased to tremble. She sat down, opened her bag and took out her cigarettes. She lit one, then she pointed to a chair away from her.

'Sit down!'

'Yes, ma'am.'

Awkwardly and sheepishly, he sat on the edge of the chair and looked down at his hands.

'Ron was real wild with me, ma'am,' he said. 'He said a blackmailer is the dirtiest thing on earth. He said I was a stinking creep to have done such a thing. I – I told him I wasn't a blackmailer. I was paid to do a job and I did it. I wouldn't blackmail anyone.' He looked up, staring miserably at her. 'He said what I had done was blackmail and he'd never speak to me again unless I came to you and explained.'

'Did you tell him who I was?' Helga asked.

He nodded.

'I guess I did. I told him everything: how you got my passport for me and about this fat guy. He said I had to help you ... so I'm here, ma'am. I've been waiting for hours here hoping you would come. I'm going to help you, ma'am.'

Helga made an impatient movement, sending her cigarette ash on the carpet.

94

'Help me? You? What do you think *you* can do? It's now much too late for anyone to help me! Now, get out! The sight of you sickens me!'

'He's got photos of us, hasn't he?'

'You know he has and he's now blackmailing me!'

'I'll get them from him, ma'am, and I'll give them to you!'

'You're talking like the fool you are! They are now out of reach. He's mailed them to his bank!'

There was a pause, then Larry said quietly, 'Is *he* out of reach, ma'am?'

There was this deadly note in his voice she had heard before when he had said to Friedlander: *What would it cost you if you got your hands crushed in a door?*

She regarded him, her body suddenly tense.

'What do you mean?'

He put his cap down on the floor beside him and took out a pack of chewing gum. As he stripped off the wrapper, he said, 'If I could get hold of him, ma'am, I could persuade him to get the photos from the bank and then you could have them.'

She pressed her hands to her face.

'You don't know what you're talking about. These photos are far too important for him to be persuaded to part with them. Just go away and leave this to me . . . you're talking nonsense.'

He fed a strip of gum in his mouth and began to chew.

'Ma'am . . . do you want me to help you?' There was an edge to his voice: a male edge which told her he was getting bored with her hysterics.

'How can you help me?' She was shrewd enough to soften her voice. 'Nothing would persuade him to part with those photographs.'

He regarded her, his Slav features without expression.

'I don't know about nothing, ma'am . . . but I could.'

Again there was this note in his voice and she looked closely at him and she felt as if an icy draught had brushed over her, leaving her cold.

'But how?'

'With these.' And he held up his huge hands. 'He's soft and fat . . . there would be no trouble.'

Her eyes opened wide as a flicker of hope came to her. Her heart began to pound.

'But the photos are in the bank by now.'

He shrugged.

'All he has to do is to write to the bank and tell them to send the photos here . . . they'd do that, wouldn't they?'

She got up, her legs unsteady, and went to the bar.

'You'd better have a drink, Larry.'

'Not for me, ma'am . . . unless you have a beer.'

She took a beer out of the refrigerator, poured it, then gave herself another vodka, adding ice and martini. While she was preparing the drinks, she was thinking.

Could this boy force Archer to sign a letter to the bank? She thought of Archer, massive, but soft and fat. She looked at Larry: built like a fighter and she could see his lumpy muscles straining against his jacket.

She handed him the beer and sat down.

'If the bank got a letter from him, they would act on his instructions,' she said, 'but he wouldn't sign.'

'He'll sign, ma'am. That's no problem.'

The way he spoke gave her hope and suddenly she felt as if a burdensome, crushing weight had been lifted off her.

'You think you can make him sign?'

He nodded.

'Yes, ma'am.'

She sipped her drink, put down the glass and lit another cigarette.

'Let me think about this, Larry.'

After a long pause, she asked, 'How long will it take you to make him sign?'

Larry considered this question as he chewed, then he shrugged.

'That's hard to say, ma'am. It depends on how stubborn he is. If he was younger, it wouldn't take long: a couple of hours, but he's getting old and he's fat and soft. I'd have to handle him carefully.' He looked up, his eyes remote. 'I'd say twenty-four hours: that's the outside limit. He'll sign before then I reckon, but let's say twenty-four hours to be on the safe side.'

She shuddered. There was something so clinical and cold

about this boy now that he was beginning to frighten her, and yet, here was the solution: a solution she couldn't afford not to accept. She had to have those photographs. She had an instinctive feeling that Archer would again dip into the account once he was sure he had her where he wanted her and she would have to lie again and again to Herman.

'I can't wait that long, Larry. My husband is arriving here the day after tomorrow. The bank will take at least a day to return the photographs. Archer will have to stay here until they arrive. We've left it too late.'

'Archer . . . is that his name, ma'am?'

'Yes. We've left it too late.'

'A problem is a challenge . . . that's what Ron always says. Can't you think of some way around this one?'

She was in the mood to face a challenge. Her mind worked swiftly and she came up with a possible solution. She looked at her watch. Her husband would be in his New York apartment clearing up final business before flying to Geneva the day after tomorrow. She got up and crossed to the telephone and dialled his New York number. There was a long pause, then she heard the ringing tone.

'This is Mr. Rolfe's residence.'

She recognized Hinkle's fruity voice.

'Oh, Hinkle, this is Mrs. Rolfe. Is my husband available?'

'No, madame. He is in conference. Is there anything I can do?'

'Yes . . . the wretched central heating system has broken down at the villa. I'm calling from the Eden hotel. There is a spare part broken and the engineer tells me the heating won't be working for at least four days. I think Mr. Rolfe should cancel his flight. He can't possibly stay in the villa . . . it's like an ice box, and you know how he detests staying at an hotel.'

'Yes, indeed, madame. You say four days ? Mr. Rolfe will be disappointed.'

'As soon as the heating is working, I will telephone.' She hesitated, then went on, 'If he decides to come in spite of this will you send me a telex at the Eden?'

'I assure you, madame, he will postpone the flight,' Hinkle said, and she drew in a quick breath of relief. She remembered Hinkle detested staying at an hotel even more than Herman did and from the tone of his voice, she was sure he would persuade Herman not to come.

'How is Mr. Rolfe?'

'Very fair, madame.'

This was Hinkle's stock answer which could mean anything.

'Then I won't expect him?'

'No, madame.'

'All right, Hinkle . . . I'll be telephoning as soon as I have news.' She hung up.

'That was smart, ma'am,' Larry said. 'You see . . . a problem is a challenge . . . Ron's right.'

She wasn't listening. She was thinking now of Archer. Here was another problem: suppose he wouldn't come to the villa? Suppose he became suspicious that she might be up to something? He held the whip hand. He could refuse to come and insist that she should come to the hotel.

As if following her thoughts, Larry said, 'How about Archer? Can you get him up here?'

'I'm not sure . . . let me think.'

She walked to the window and looked down at the lake, her mind busy. The whole plan would be defeated if Archer refused to come and he might well refuse. She would refuse if she were in his place. Why should he come? He had said she was dangerous. She felt suddenly sure that he wouldn't come, but he would insist she brought the stock list to the hotel . . . unless she could trick him into coming.

She moved away from the window, picked up a cigarette and lit it. She was aware that Larry was watching her. She looked at her wristwatch. The time was 12.05. There was a chance Archer would have returned to the hotel for a pre-lunch cocktail. He was expecting her to call at 15.00. She decided the only way to trap him was to bustle him into coming so he would have no time for caution nor to suspect this could be a trap.

A fidgeting movement from Larry broke her concentration. She looked impatiently at him.

'Excuse me, ma'am. I could do with something to eat. Is there anything to eat?'

She pressed her hand to her forehead.

'For God's sake, don't bother me ... I'm trying to think. Go to the kitchen and help yourself!'

'Thank you, ma'am.'

As he left the room she sat down and picked up her drink. She sat still, her mind concentrating on the problem. Finally, after ten minutes of thought, she came up with a possible solution. Considering this solution, she was now fairly satisfied that she could get Archer to come to the villa. But once he was there, would Larry be able to handle him? He seemed certain he could, but suppose Archer refused to sign the letter? He might have more steel in him than he appeared to have. If Larry failed, Archer would take his revenge. Then she remembered the deadly note in Larry's voice and the remote, cold look in his eyes when he said: *He's soft and fat. That would be no problem.*

Sink or swim, Archer had said. Well, she too wasn't the sinking type.

'It's all ready, ma'am,' Larry said coming to the door. 'Come on ... you gotta eat.'

'I don't want anything.'

'Oh, come on, ma'am. We could have a rough afternoon. Have you thought of something?'

'Yes.'

'Fine ... let's eat.'

Shrugging she went with him into the kitchen. He had made a vast bowl of spaghetti, using the peeled tomatoes, the tomato purée and the onions she had bought.

It looked so appetising that she suddenly felt hungry. Together, in silence, they demolished the pasta.

'You're quite a cook, Larry.'

He gave her his warm, friendly smile.

'Yeah ... I'm not bad ... my Ma taught me.' He wiped his mouth with the back of his hand. 'When are you getting him up here, ma'am?'

She stood up, pushing the kitchen chair away from her.

'If he's coming ... in about half an hour.'

She went into the living-room for a cigarette. Larry followed her.

'Any idea how he will come, ma'am?'

'He has a hired car.'

As Larry stripped the wrapping from a piece of gum, she lit her cigarette.

'Do you think if I opened the garage door, he'd drive in?'

She looked at him, puzzled.

'Why do you ask?'

'Well, ma'am, it would be best if we did the talking in the games room downstairs.' He looked around the elegantly furnished room. 'This is a nice room. It would be a shame to mess it up.'

Again she felt as if an icy draught had blown around her.

'You're not going to ... hurt him?'

'I don't know, ma'am. I hope not.' He smiled. 'But some of these elderly finks think they are younger than they are. I might have to smack him a couple of times. I don't reckon I'll have to, but if I did and he fell over, the best place for him to fall over would be in the games room, wouldn't it?'

Suddenly, she felt slightly sick.

'He's no fool, Larry. I couldn't persuade him to go down to the games room. He would immediately suspect something.'

Larry chewed and thought about this.

'Yeah ... well, that's okay. I won't smack him so hard then. If I have to soften him, I'll take him down to the games room. So maybe we'd better not waste any more time, ma'am. Will you get him up here?'

She hesitated for a few moments. Should she do this? Was she bringing further disaster on herself? Then she remembered Archer's merciless eyes as he had said: *Decision? You have no choice! I have you where I want you!*

She went to the telephone and dialled the number of the Eden hotel.

'Is Mr. Archer in the hotel, please?'

'A moment, madame.'

She waited several moments.

'Hello, yes? Who's that?' Archer's voice boomed over the line. She could tell by the pitch of his voice that he was on his third cocktail.

'Jack! I have to see you! Something's happened!' She put urgency in her voice.

'Is that you, Helga?'

'Yes ... of course! Will you come to the villa at once?'

'What do you mean? I'm about to have lunch.' All the charm had gone from his voice now. 'We have an appointment at three and I'm expecting you here.'

'I'm catching a train to Milan in two hours, Jack. I'm flying back to New York tonight.'

'What the hell are you talking about?' She caught an uncertain note in his voice.

'Don't ask questions, Jack. We're on an open line. Hinkle has just telephoned. There is an emergency. It's bad. I'm flying back tonight.'

'Good God! Is it ...?'

'Jack!' Her scream cut him short. 'Not on an open line. Hinkle says it is touch and go. Not a word, Jack! This could upset the market ... it could plunge ... will you come?'

'You damn well bet I'm coming! Be with you in ten minutes,' and the line went dead.

Slowly she replaced the receiver: a surge of triumph running through her. It had been an inspired thought and it had worked. She had conveyed to Archer that Herman was either dying or dead. She had mentioned the Stock Market. That would stop him trying to check if it was a lie or not. She knew even the slightest rumour that Herman was ill would send prices plunging. For Archer, this would be the time to sell before the news hit the headlines, then when the market had absorbed the shock, to buy back. He would also realize as he came storming up the St. Moritz highway that with Herman dead, he would lose his power over Helga. He would be in the mood to try to make a bargain.

She looked at Larry.

'It worked,' she said breathlessly. 'He's coming.'

Alone, Helga stood by the window that overlooked the private road leading to the villa, a cigarette burning in her fingers. Her heart was thumping and she felt cold in spite of the heating. She was committed now: there was no turning back. She hated violence. She could never bear to see violence on the movies or the TV screen and yet she knew there would be violence here this afternoon. She knew once Archer realized he had been tricked he would be like a raging, vicious bull. She had no doubt that Larry, a much younger and fitter man could cope with him, but the thought of what was to come sickened her.

Larry had said he would stay out of sight until Archer was in the living-room.

'Talk to him first, ma'am. Maybe you can persuade him to play ball. I'll be listening. If you can't, then I'll take over.'

She looked at her watch. He would be here any minute now. At this hour, the traffic would be heavy, but once past Cassarate, unless he got stuck behind the local bus, he could speed.

Then she saw the Fiat 125 sweep into sight, driving much too fast. She caught a glimpse of Archer as she stepped away from the window.

'He's here, Larry.' Her voice was unsteady.

'Okay, ma'am. You've got nothing to worry about,' Larry said from the kitchen. 'I'm right with you.'

She heard a car door slam, then the front door bell rang violently.

'Be careful with him, Larry,' she said.

'That's okay, ma'am. You've got nothing to worry about.'

Again the front door bell rang.

Bracing herself, she crossed the hall and opened the door. Archer bounded in. His heavy face was pale and his eyes had an unnatural glitter.

'Is he dead?' he demanded.

Helga looked stonily at him, turned and walked to the sitting-room. She heard Archer curse under his breath. In the doorway, she paused.

'Take your coat off, Jack ... it's hot in here. I wouldn't want you to catch a cold.'

As he tore off his coat and flung it on the hall table, he said again, 'Helga! Is he dead?'

She moved into the room until she reached the centre, then turned and faced him as he came in.

'Helga! For Christ's sake! Is he dead?'

'Is who dead?'

His big hands closed into fists and he glared at her.

'You said there was an emergency ... that Hinkle telephoned!'

'Oh, yes. Hinkle did telephone. Herman won't be coming here until next week. He's got some conference on or some bore.'

A wary, suspicious look came to Archer's face.

'Just what is this? You led me to believe Herman was ill or dead.'

'Did I? Perhaps it was because I decided there would be no other way of getting you up here, Jack.'

His face turned mauve as blood rushed to his head.

'Listen, you bitch, don't start any tricks!' he snarled. 'Those photos are now safe in the bank! With a snap of my fingers I can ruin you and you know it! Now give me the stock list! I've about had all I'm taking from you! Give me the stock list!'

She moved to a chair and sat down.

'The situation has changed, Jack. You're not getting the list, but you are writing a letter to your bank, instructing them to send the photos to me.'

He glared at her, his mouth working.

'I've a good mind to slap your bloody face!' he said viciously. 'Have you gone out of your mind? Or are you telling me you don't give a damn about losing sixty million dollars?'

'The situation has changed,' she repeated quietly, feeling her anger rising. 'You held three aces ... but now I hold four.'

He suddenly appeared to take hold of himself and his face was no longer mauve. He stared at her, his small, hard eyes probing.

'That's interesting. You were always a good bluffer, Helga, but you don't bluff me. If I have any more of your nonsense, I will instruct my bank to send that envelope immediately to Herman! I'm calling your bluff.'

'If you do that, you go to jail.'

'Listen, you stupid bitch, can't you see I have no alternative? I'm willing to bet against my chance of going to jail against your chances of inheriting sixty million dollars,' Archer said. 'I'll give you two minutes to give me that stock list or I leave here and when I get back to Lausanne I give you my word the photos go to Herman!'

'Your word?' She smiled bitterly. 'What's that worth?'

'You wait and see!'

He shot his cuff and regarded his watch.

'Two minutes!'

'Jack ... will you please write to the bank and ask them to send me the photos? I'm asking this for your sake as well as mine,' Helga said.

'One minute!'

She lifted her hands and in despair, dropped them in her lap.

He pulled his cuff over his watch.

'Okay, Helga. That's it. So we're no longer partners. The photos will be delivered to Herman as he leaves Geneva airport. I'll be able to put up with life in a prison cell, thinking of you booted out of your comfortable nest.'

He turned and marched to the door, jerked it open and found himself confronted by Larry.

He reared back as if he had touched a live cable, stumbled and had to make an effort to regain his balance.

Larry moved into the room, his jaw moving rhythmically, his hands in his jeans pockets.

'Hi, Fatso,' he said in his quiet drawl. 'Remember me?'

'What are you doing here?' Archer snarled. He whirled around, glaring at Helga. 'Is this your doing?'

'You shouldn't have done this to me,' Helga said quietly. 'You should have known you couldn't get away with blackmailing me. Now, write to the bank and tell them to send the photos.' She pointed to the desk. 'Do it at once!'

'I'll see you damned first!' Archer snarled. 'You don't think this pimp of yours frightens me?'

Larry reached out, grabbed Archer's arm and spun him around. His open right hand, moving so fast it looked to Helga like a blur of white, slapped Archer's face. The sound of his palm against Archer's fat jowl was like a pistol shot. She saw something fly out of Archer's mouth as he staggered back. She looked down. Archer's top denture lay at her feet: six gleaming white teeth set on a gold plate. She shut her eyes and turned away.

She heard Archer mumble something, then Larry, his voice sounding deadly, said, 'Stay right where you are or I'll tread on them!'

She braced herself and turned.

A livid red mark showed on Archer's face. He looked changed without his top teeth and his lips had fallen in. To her, he looked old, stupid and frightened.

Larry had moved to where the denture had fallen. There was a hard grin on his face as he watched Archer.

'There's plenty of the same unless you do what you're told.'

Archer made a whinnying sound, then turning, he charged out of the room into the hall. Larry went after him, moving silently and swiftly.

The slapping sound came again. Helga stood motionless, fighting down the bile rising in her mouth. She heard Archer suddenly cry out. It was a horrible sound and she put her hands over her ears, but her hands couldn't keep out the savage sound going on in the hall: the tramping of feet, the quick in-take of breath, the inhuman grunting of a man trying to exert all his strength, then the sound of a heavy fall that shook the villa.

She rushed to the open door.

Archer was lying on his back and Larry was standing over him. As she paused, Larry kicked the prostrated man in his ribs, shifting his heavy body by the force of his kick and making Archer cry out.

'Stop it! Stop it!' Helga cried. 'Larry! Stop it!'

He frowned, looked blankly at her, and for a moment he didn't seem to recognize her, then his face relaxed and he grinned, stepping back.

'He's okay, ma'am ... just trying to be younger than he is.'

'Leave him alone!'

'Sure, ma'am.' Larry moved further away, then looking

down at Archer, he said, 'Come on, Fatso, get up. You're not hurt . . . yet. Come on.'

Very slowly, Archer crawled to his feet. He staggered to the wall and leaned against it, breathing heavily and sagging at the knees. The right side of his face now showed a black bruise, tinged with red and a trickle of blood ran from the side of his mouth.

Helga looked away. The sight of his face sickened her.

'That's the boy,' Larry said. 'Now go in there and collect your teeth, then write that letter.'

Archer glared at him, then at Helga.

'By God! I'll make you two pay for this,' he mumbled. He pulled out a handkerchief and dabbed the blood from his mouth. The spite and viciousness in his eyes chilled Helga.

'Sure . . . sure,' Larry said softly. 'We know all about that. Go ahead . . . get in there!'

Unsteadily and moving like a cripple, Archer walked into the sitting-room. He picked up his denture and put it in his mouth.

'Maybe, ma'am, you'd better write the letter. I don't reckon he's up to it,' Larry said, eyeing Archer.

'Yes,' Helga said.

'Sit down,' Larry said to Archer. 'Take it easy.'

Archer sank into a chair and held his face in his hands. His breathing was very laboured and alarmed Helga.

'Is he all right?'

'Oh, sure, ma'am . . . he's fine. Don't worry about him,' Larry said. 'You get that letter written.'

Helga went to the desk, took a portable Olivetti from one of the bottom drawers and put it on the desk. Her hands were shaking a little, and the paper rattled as she threaded it into the typewriter. She hesitated for a long moment, breathing deeply until she regained some composure, then she began to type.

The only sound in the big room was the clacking of the typewriter and Archer's laboured breathing.

Larry stripped a stick of chewing gum and put it in his mouth.

It took Helga only a few minutes to complete the letter.
She ripped the sheet out of the typewriter and checked what
she had written.

Villa Helios
Castagnola 6976

The Manager,
Central Bank of Vaud.
Lausanne. 1003.

Dear Sir,
Yesterday, I mailed to you an envelope marked 'To be
opened in the event of my death.'
I now find I need to make additions to the document contained in the second sealed envelope. Will you please return
this envelope, unopened, to me by registered and express mail
at the above address. Your immediate action will oblige.
Yours truly,
John Lee Archer

She put the letter on the desk and looked at Archer who
still sat motionless, his face in his hands.
'Jack ...'
He didn't move and Larry, frowning, gave him a hard
poke in his back with his finger.
'The lady's speaking to you, buster,' he said.
Archer looked up slowly and her heart sank when she saw
the expression in his eyes. She saw then he had more steel in
him than she had imagined. He had absorbed the first shock,
and now his bruised face was set and his eyes glittered with
the viciousness of a cornered animal.
'I'll read the letter to you,' she said.
He pressed his hand to his aching face and continued to
glare at her.
Her voice a little husky, she read the letter aloud. He just
sat there, now staring down at the carpet and mopping at his
bleeding mouth.
'Will you sign it?' she asked.
He looked up.
'I forged your signature ... go ahead and forge mine.' The

hate in his eyes sickened her. 'Go ahead and see how far it'll get you.'

Larry made a slight movement towards him, but Helga gestured to him to stay where he was.

'Jack . . . I told you I hold four aces. You'll sign sooner or later. I must have those photographs,' she said, her hands into fists on the desk. 'I hate this. I want to spare you although you don't deserve any consideration, but I do want to spare you. Please sign this letter.'

'You and your pimp can go to hell!' Archer snarled. 'As long as I have those photographs I'm safe . . . without them, I'm not.'

'If you sign this letter Jack, and I get the photos, I give you my solemn promise that Herman won't prosecute, but you'll have to lose the account. I promise you won't go to prison.'

'What's your promise worth to me? It's stalemate, you bitch. I'm not signing.'

'Larry promised me he would make you sign,' Helga said, trying desperately to quell the panic and despair rising in her. 'That means he will ill-treat you. For God's sake, Jack! I don't want you hurt. Please sign this letter!'

Archer stared at her, his eyes narrowing.

'I told you . . . it's stalemate! If this ape starts knocking me about, he could kill me. "In the event of my death" . . . remember? I'll tell you something I haven't told anyone. I have a bad heart. My quack warned me on no account was I to over-exert myself. So go ahead if you want me dead. Tell your ape to start knocking me about.'

Larry, chewing gum, was listening to all this, his eyes shifting from Helga to Archer and back to Helga again. He saw the dismay growing in Helga's eyes and he moved into action.

He went up to Archer.

'Up on your feet!' he said. 'You and me are going downstairs. Come on.'

'No!' Helga's voice was shrill. 'Don't touch him!'

'It's okay, ma'am. I'm not touching him unless I have to. I want to talk to him. On your feet, buster.'

Archer stood up.

'Keep away from me! I'm walking out of here and I'm daring either of you to stop me! Now, get out of my way!'

With a movement like a striking snake, Larry's big hand closed over Archer's wrist, twisted, had Archer spinning around and then bending his arm he had him in a paralysing grip.

Helga jumped to her feet.

'Larry! No!'

'It's okay,' Larry said quietly. 'He doesn't want to drop dead, do you, Fatso? Move with the legs.'

Her heart hammering, Helga watched Larry march Archer out of the room. She heard them going down the stairs and she walked unsteadily to an armchair and sank into it and put her hands to her face.

Her bluff had been called. From the moment she had agreed to let Larry help her, she had a feeling it would end in disaster. She dare not risk Archer dying. It would be better to submit to his blackmail. Jumping to her feet, she ran into the hall and paused as she saw Larry coming up the stairs from the cellars.

'What have you done with him?'

'He's okay, ma'am. I've locked him in one of the cellars . . . the one at the far end . . . the empty one. He can't get out. I thought maybe you and me ought to have a talk before we do anything more.'

She went back into the sitting-room.

'We must let him go, Larry.'

'Do you think he's bluffing about his bad heart, ma'am?'

She lifted her hands helplessly.

'How do I know? He looks like a man with heart trouble. I don't know, but if you try to force him to sign and he dies . . . no, Larry, we can't do it.'

Larry rubbed the back of his neck.

'Mind if I have a beer, ma'am?'

'No . . . help yourself . . . have anything!'

He went over to the bar, opened the refrigerator, took out a bottle of beer.

'This is pretty handy, isn't it, ma'am? You've certainly got it all laid on. Do you want something?'

'No.'

She sat in despair, trying to think of a way out and finding none.

I'll make you two pay for this!

He would, of course. He knew Larry was an Army deserter. He would inform against him. Herself? He would be merciless, bleeding the account with impunity, making her cover up his embezzlement.

'Look, ma'am, take it easy,' Larry said. He carried his glass of beer from the bar and sat down opposite her. 'We can still fix this. Have you got a copy of his signature?'

She stiffened and looked quickly at him.

'Yes, but I could never forge it.'

'Could I see it, ma'am?'

'But why? I don't understand.'

'Could I see it, ma'am?'

She went to the desk, found a file containing the dozens of letters Archer had written to her concerning business transactions. She looked at the almost indecipherable signature. No . . . to forge that wasn't possible.

She handed one of the letters to Larry who looked at it.

'A real mean signature, isn't it, ma'am?'

'Yes, but his bank knows it. It is impossible to forge.'

'Maxie could do it with his eyes shut.'

She stiffened.

'Who?'

'Maxie Friedlander . . . the guy who fixed my passport. He could do it.'

The feeling of utter defeat and despair that was crushing her lifted.

'Would he?'

Larry smiled his warm, friendly smile.

'From what Ron tells me, ma'am, Maxie would cut his own throat if the money was right. Yeah . . . he'd do it.'

'He wouldn't ask questions?'

'No, ma'am.'

'But he would have to see the letter, Larry. It gives my address. He could blackmail me.'

'He needn't see the letter. You could cover it up. Anyway, Maxie wouldn't want trouble. You pay him enough and there'll be no kick-back.'

'How much would he want?'

'I don't know that, ma'am. Maybe what you paid him for my passport. I'll get it as cheap as I can.'

She leaned forward, clasping her hands.

'Will you do it?'

'Why, sure, ma'am. Ron told me I was to help you and that's what I'm going to do. Give me the money and I'll go now if you'll let me have your car. I reckon it'll take me a little over five hours to get to Basle.' He looked at the ornate clock on the overmantel. 'It's now nearly two o'clock. I'll be with Maxie around seven o'clock. Maybe he'll take an hour for the job. I'll be back here by two in the morning. How's that?'

Again she had the feeling of pending disaster, but she could think of no other alternative.

'Thank you, Larry. Take the car. What about . . . him?'

'I'll fix him up before I go. He'll want something to eat and a bucket to pee in. You leave all this to me. I'll be off in half an hour.'

He went briskly into the kitchen.

She sat there for some moments, trying to convince herself that this new plan could save her, but she was too shaken and uneasy to think coherently. She got up and went into the kitchen to find Larry boiling four eggs and defrosting bread in the oven.

'This will keep him going, ma'am, until I get back. Keep away from him. I'll be as quick as I can.'

'Don't take risks, Larry. For God's sake, don't have an accident.'

'I'll watch it, ma'am. Will you get the letter ready?'

'Yes.'

She went back to the sitting-room, found two sheets of typing paper and put the letter between them, leaving room for the signature space to protrude. She taped the two sheets together, completely concealing the letter. She folded it carefully and put it in a large envelope.

It would mean another day's delay, she thought. She had to see the letter before she posted it to the Bank. She had to be sure the signature would be acceptable.

Then she went into the room. Herman used as a study,

pushed back one of the oak panels to reveal a small safe. She spun the dial, opened the safe and took from it a leather folder. From the folder, she counted our forty one hundred franc notes. Returning the folder and relocking the safe, she went back to the sitting-room.

'Larry?'

As he didn't reply, she went to the kitchen, but he wasn't there. She went to the top of the stairs leading to the cellar. She could hear him talking. Moving quietly, she went down a few of the stairs to hear better.

She heard him say, 'Make yourself at home, Fatso. You've got food now and it won't be long before we let you go. Just take it easy.'

She heard a door slam, then Larry came running along the passage, pausing when he saw her. He grinned.

'Nothing to worry about, ma'am. Just keep clear of him. He can't get out. I'll get going. You got the letter?'

They climbed the stairs together and went into the sitting-room.

'Here's four thousand francs, Larry. Do you think it'll be enough?'

'Yeah, ma'am. I'll talk him into it. Sure, it's more than enough.'

'And here's the letter.'

She took the letter from the envelope and showed him how she had concealed the letter.

'Stay with him while he does it, Larry. Make sure he doesn't see what's written here.'

'You bet, ma'am.'

She put her hand on his arm.

'And thank you, Larry, for all you're doing for me.'

He smiled.

'Thank you, ma'am for giving me the chance to put things right. Don't you worry ... I'll fix it. See you around two tonight.'

'Don't take risks.'

'I won't. Well, so long, ma'am ... be seeing you,' and he went out of the living-room, out into the hall, snatched up his baseball cap, then opening the front door, he ran down the steps to the garage.

Standing by the big window, Helga watched him drive down the grit strewn road until the car disappeared from sight.

She suddenly felt very alone.

CHAPTER SIX

FOR some moments, Helga stood thinking. There must be no loose strings, she told herself. Had Archer checked out of the Eden hotel? It would be awkward if the hotel began an inquiry. Then she remembered he had booked an air taxi to take him back to Lausanne.

She knew Toni Hoffman, the secretary of the Flying Club at Agno. Quickly she looked up the telephone number and in minutes, was speaking to Hoffman.

As soon as she introduced herself, he became friendly and attentive.

'A wonderful surprise, Madame Rolfe! Are you needing a plane?'

'No, but my husband will be arriving next week. Mr. Hoffman, I believe Mr. Archer has chartered an air taxi?'

'Mr. Archer? Yes . . . that's right. He's due to take off in an hour.'

'Would you please cancel the flight? Mr. Archer has been detained. He will, of course, cover the cost. When he is ready to leave, he will make another reservation.'

'Certainly, Madame Rolfe. I'll tell the pilot. How is Mr. Rolfe?'

They chatted for a few minutes, then Helga hung up.

Should she call the Eden hotel? She thought for a moment. If there was a suitcase in Archer's car she would know he had checked out. Slipping on her coat, she left the villa and went to the garage. She found a suitcase lying on the back seat of the Fiat. So he had checked out, she thought as she closed the garage door.

Then she remembered it was possible that Herman might send her a Telex. He had a mania about sending messages by Telex. She had to be sure the Eden didn't Telex back that she had checked out.

She returned to the villa and called the Eden. As soon as she was put through to the Reception Manager, she asked if there had been a Telex from her husband.

'No, Madame Rolfe. Are you expecting one?'

'It is possible. If one comes would you be kind enough to telephone me? I am at my villa.'

'Certainly, madame . . . a pleasure.'

Again she stood thinking. Knowing how busy Archer always was it was certain his secretary had set up appointments for him the following day. She must stop her making inquiries. She hesitated, then dialled Archer's office number.

While she waited for a reply, she calculated how long Archer would have to remain under lock and key. When Larry returned, she would drive to Lugano's Central Post Office and post the letter to catch the first mail out. The letter wouldn't reach the Bank until the following morning. The Bank would post the envelope to the villa the same day and it would arrive the following morning. Say three days. Today was Tuesday. To be on the safe side, she would say Archer wouldn't be back in Lausanne until Sunday evening.

A moment later he was speaking to Betty Brownlow who had worked under her when she had been Archer's personal assistant and who had taken over from her when she had married Herman.

'Hello Betty, this is Helga.'

'Why, Helga, how nice to hear your voice again. How are you?'

They chatted for a few moments, then Betty said, 'Have you seen Jack? He is in Lugano.'

'Yes . . . that's why I'm phoning. Something important has come up. My husband has sent a Telex. He has asked Jack to go to Rome to fix a deal. Jack asked me to call you to cancel all his appointments. He won't be back until Sunday night.'

'He's gone to Rome? But he can't have!'

Helga stiffened and her heart missed a beat.

'He has. What do you mean?'

'He hasn't his passport with him!'

115

Helga flinched. Fool! Not to have thought of that. Why hadn't she said Archer had gone to Zurich?

'Are you sure?' She forced her voice to sound casual.

'Yes. His passport is in my drawer. I asked him if he wanted it and he said he didn't.'

Helga forced her mind to work.

'It'll be all right. The last time I went to Milan I forgot my passport. There was a bit of a fuss, but they accepted my driving licence. Jack will manage.'

'Do you think so?' A pause, then Betty went on, her voice worried, 'He usually stops at the Grand. I could post the passport to him express. He might get it tomorrow. It would save a fuss when he leaves.'

God! Helga thought, couldn't this woman stop being so damned efficient?

'Not the Grand,' she said. 'He phoned ... they're full. He is taking pot luck. Don't send the passport, Betty. He would be furious if it got lost. I'd forget it ... I know he will manage.'

'Well ... if you think so. Anyway he will be telephoning me. He always does when he's away and I can ask him what to do.'

Helga closed her eyes, then opened them. She should have thought of that too.

'I don't think you will hear from him, Betty. He's going to be very busy. In fact he told me to tell you not to worry if you don't hear from him.'

'Not hear from him?' Betty's voice became alarmed. 'But I have a mass of queries I have to ask him about!'

Helga had had enough of this.

'That's what he said, darling. You'll manage ... I always did. 'bye now,' and she hung up.

Her hands were moist and she sat for some moments trying to convince herself that she had convinced Betty. She decided there was nothing Betty could do. At least she wouldn't be alarmed and start making inquiries.

What else had she to do? Then she remembered that the cleaning woman would be arriving the following morning. Still another telephone call. She found the number, called the cleaning agency and told them to stop the woman from coming. She said she would telephone again when she wanted the woman.

She lit a cigarette and looked at her watch. The time was now 15.50. She thought of the long hours ahead of her. She thought of Larry speeding towards Basle. She hoped he wouldn't have an accident. The road to the Bernadino tunnel was narrow, twisting and dangerous. She told herself firmly she mustn't worry about him. He was an expert driver and he knew the risks.

Then she thought of Archer locked in the small cellar. At least there was a light and a radiator. He wouldn't freeze. She wondered what he was thinking. Had he guessed she would try to forge his signature? It had been his own suggestion. Was he in pain? She thought of the brutal kick Larry had given him and she flinched. Had he really a bad heart? So many fat men had bad hearts these days, but it could have been a clever bluff just to stop Larry hitting him again. Archer had always been quick thinking and an expert bluffer. It was probably bluff. She hoped it was.

She looked around the big room rather helplessly, wondering how she could occupy herself for the next twelve hours. There was some intricate tapestry work she had brought with her, but she knew she couldn't settle to that. She switched on the television set. A long-haired youth, howling into a microphone, swam into view and she hurriedly turned the knob to catch the German station. A fat man was talking about future plans for education and impatiently, she tried the Italian station: only the test chart greeted her and she turned the set off.

She wandered around the room. The light was fading and the sun, setting behind the mountain, made an impressive splash of red in the sky. It had stopped snowing. For something to do, she lowered the shutters and pulled the drapes. She then went into her bedroom and did the same thing there.

She looked around the elegant room, then remembered that Larry would be hungry when he returned. She must get something out of the freezer for him.

She went into the kitchen, opened the freezer and looked at the neatly packaged assortment of food it contained. She finally decided on a fillet of pork. That, with a packet of peas and a packet of chip potatoes should satisfy his hunger. She put the food on the kitchen table to defrost.

Then as she was leaving the kitchen, she paused, her heart suddenly racing.

A heavy pounding sound was coming from the cellars!

For a moment she stood rooted, her heart hammering so violently she had trouble in breathing.

Archer!

God! If he breaks out! she thought.

In panic, she ran to the head of the stairs leading to the cellar. The noise he was making now terrified her. He was kicking steadily against the door. He could break out!

She paused, then steeling herself, clutching hold of the banister rail, she went down, stopping at the foot of the stairs to look along the passage.

She remembered the cellar door opened outwards. From where she stood, she could see the door shaking under the steady, pounding thuds. She sped along the passage, past the quivering door and locked the steel door, leading to the garage. She took out the key. She stood staring at the cellar door and her panic increased as she saw there was a split in one of the panels.

'Jack!' she screamed.

The thudding ceased.

'Let me out of here!' Archer's voice sounded breathless and vicious. 'Do you hear? Let me out!'

She forced down her panic.

'Stop it! You're not getting out!' Her voice sounded to her unnaturally shrill. 'If you wake Larry, he'll come down and I won't be responsible!'

'Is he in your bed, you bitch?'

'I warn you! If you go on making that noise, he'll come down!'

Through the cracked panel she could hear his heavy breathing.

'Let him! He daren't touch me and you know it! You wouldn't dare let him touch me!'

'I would! I know you're lying about your heart! If you don't stop this, he'll come down!'

'By God! I'll make you pay for this!'

'Shut up! If you make any more noise, I'll wake Larry and send him down to you!'

'Damn you to hell!'

Shaking, she walked along the passage and up the stairs. She locked the door leading to the cellars and took the key. She went into the living-room and put the two keys on the overmantel.

She waited, listening, but now she could hear only the muffled roar of the central heating motor. She drew in a deep breath of relief. Her threat ... her bluff ... had worked! Then she thought of that split panel. If she hadn't gone down and stopped him, he would have broken out. Well, now, if he did get out of the cellar he would have to batter down the door to the hall. He would never hope to open the steel door leading to the garage. While there was time, should she do something about the door leading to the hall?

She went into the hall and looked at the door. It didn't seem to her to appear very strong: one powerful kick might easily smashed it open.

There was a heavy iron bound Medici chest standing under the window: yet another of her husband's collector's pieces. She dragged this across the door. It would be better than nothing, she told herself. She now felt so shaky, she went into the sitting-room and poured herself a large brandy.

She sat down. She was sipping the brandy when the telephone bell rang. The sound so startled her she slopped some of her drink. Hastily putting down the glass, she crossed to the telephone and picked up the receiver.

It was the Reception Manager of the Eden hotel.

'Madame Rolfe ... a telex has just come in for you. Would you like me to send someone up to you with it?'

Now what? she wondered, flinching.

'No ... no ... please read it to me.'

'It's from Mr. Rolfe. It says: "Have instructed expert to fix central heating. He promises action this night. No wish to cancel my flight. Telephone me when fixed".'

Helga turned cold.

'Would you like me to repeat that, madame?'

'No, thank you. I have it. Thank you for calling,' and she hung up.

The grandfather clock that had cost Herman Rolfe more than six thousand dollars began to chime.

Helga glanced at her watch. The time was 21.25. The Grandfather clock was a collector's piece and wasn't expected to keep faithful time.

Since Herman's telex, Helga had sat with a blank mind, waiting for the central heating engineer. She was now beginning to think he wasn't coming. There had been no sound from Archer. Her threat seemed to have cowed him. She had smoked innumerable cigarettes and she had drunk another brandy. She was feeling slightly light-headed, but in spite of the heat from the radiators, she felt cold.

She had pulled up the shutter covering the smaller of the three windows and had pulled back the drapes. The distant lights of Lugano and the two red warning lights on the TV and radio masts on top of the mountain helped against the growing feeling of claustrophobia.

Then she heard the noisy engine of an approaching car. She went to the window. She saw a Volkswagen, snow on its roof, pull up by the front door and a man get out. He leaned into the car and took from it a heavy tool case which he slung over his shoulder.

She braced herself and went to the front door just as he rang. As she opened the door, an icy blast greeted her, making her shiver. She had had no idea it had turned so cold and her mind flew to Larry.

'Schroder . . . heating engineers,' the man said in Italian. She could see the puzzled expression in his eyes as he felt the warmth coming from the hall. 'You have trouble here, madame?'

'Come in.' She couldn't bear the cold for a moment longer. The freezing air cut into her like a knife.

He stepped into the hall and she closed the door.

'I'm sorry Mr. Rolfe called you,' she said. 'When I arrived, I couldn't get the heating to work. I was being stupid. It's working perfectly now. I'm so sorry.'

120

The Engineer, a middle-aged, heavy-faced Swiss, smiled cheerfully.

'That's all right, madame. The great thing is it's working. My boss was worried. He didn't want you to freeze up. Mr. Rolfe was threatening to sue us.'

Helga forced a smile.

'Mr. Rolfe is always threatening to sue someone ... he never does.'

'While I'm here, madame, I'll check the motor. My boss wants to send a telex back to Mr. Rolfe.'

'No ... don't bother.' It would be far too dangerous to let him down to the cellars. She spoke hurried. 'It's working perfectly. I – I was just being stupid. I forgot to press the right button. I can't think why I forgot.'

The Engineer shifted the sling of his bag.

'It's no bother ... it's my job.' Then she saw a puzzled look come into his eyes. He was looking at the chest pulled across the door to the cellars. She knew he had been here before and knew the geography of the villa.

'I'm sorry,' she said firmly. 'It is not convenient. I am very tired and I was just going to bed when you arrived. Wait a moment.' She went quickly to her bedroom and with shaking hands, she opened her purse and took out a fifty franc note. Then as she was leaving the room, she heard the heavy thudding sounds from the cellars.

Archer, she thought, panic seizing her, must have heard the front door bell ring and with new courage, was attacking the door again.

When she regained the hall, she found the Engineer was examining the chest. The thudding sound from below created such a din that it set Helga's teeth on edge. Somehow she kept her face expressionless.

'Please take this. Thank you for coming. I'm telephoning my husband. There is no need for you to go to the expense of sending him a telex. I'll explain everything ... it is entirely my mistake.'

His eyes opened wide when he saw the fifty franc note.

'Thank you, madame ... thank you very much.' His eyes went to the cellar door. The thudding sound was now alarmingly loud.

'A friend of mine . . . he's making something,' Helga said huskily and opened the front door.

'Well, madame, if you're sure . . .'

'Yes. It's working perfectly!'

He moved out into the cold.

'Good night, madame, and thank you.'

As she closed the front door, she heard a sudden sound of splintering wood and then a crash as the cellar door slammed open and banged against the wall.

She clenched her fists.

He was out!

Her breath rasping in her throat, she looked at the heavy chest against the door. Would that be enough to stop him forcing the door open? Then as she heard Archer come pounding up the stairs she also heard the engine of the Volkswagen whirr into life and the car drive away.

She leaned against the wall, staring at the door. She could hear Archer's laboured breathing, then she saw the door handle turn.

'Jack! Get away from that door!' she cried. 'This is your last chance! Get away from that door or I'll call Larry!'

'He's not here,' Archer panted. 'I know! You can't bluff me! I heard the car and I know where he's gone . . . he's gone to Basle! Open up or I'll break the door down! Do you hear? Open the door!'

She stared at the door. How could she make it safe? Then she remembered a scaffolding pole the builder had forgotten that was in the garage.

She ran to the front door, opened it and stumbled down the steps to the garage. The cold bit into her, but she ignored it. She opened the garage doors, found the pole and caught hold if it. It was heavy and clumsy to handle but she carried it back up the steps and into the hall.

She paused to stare at the door. The lock was now broken and the door was open an inch, but the chest was holding it. She could hear Archer's heavy breathing as he paused for his final effort. Would the pole be too long? Her own breathing was laboured. She wedged one end of the pole against the skirting of the opposite wall, then lowered the other end against the door. She gave a little sob of relief as she saw it was a fit. She jammed the pole down, forcing the door shut.

Archer made his effort and she heard his body thud against the door. The pole held the door solid and she heard his gasp of pain as his shoulder crashed against the door which didn't yield.

She heard him curse. The step at the door wasn't wide enough to give him much purchase. He wouldn't be able to use his foot, she thought. He would soon get tired of bruising his shoulder.

'You bitch!' Archer snarled. 'Open the door!'

She went into the kitchen to where the tool chest was kept. Herman was a great believer in having tools in all his homes. He never used them himself but expected Hinkle to cope with any small emergency. She found a heavy, wooden mallet and with that, standing on a chair, she hammered the pole more securely into place.

While she was working, Archer called her every obscene name that came to his mind.

Dropping the mallet, now sure the door was safe, she went unsteadily into the sitting-room. Again she looked at her watch. She had still three – possibly four – hours before Larry returned.

Now she had to persuade Herman to cancel his flight. It wouldn't do to telephone him. He would only argue. If she couldn't persuade him to cancel his flight he would be arriving at Geneva the following evening and at Agno airport the morning of the next day. This was too dangerous. She had to keep him away from the villa for at least another three days.

She listened, but heard no sound from the cellars, then she went to her desk and sat down. After thinking, she decided to ask the Eden to send a telex. Herman had a secretary at his New York apartment who would accept the message if Herman was out.

She wrote the message out on a sheet of paper.

Central heating now working, but villa still like ice box. Will take at least a day to warm up. Cleaners have been unable to work, due to cold. They arrive Thursday morning. Suggest you fly to Geneva Friday. I will meet you at Agno

Saturday usual time. Think all will be ready by then. Snowing heavily here, Helga.

She re-read the message, decided Hinkle would be consulted and would veto flying tomorrow, then she rang the Eden and dictated the message to the clerk in charge of the telex. He promised to send the message immediately.

As she replaced the receiver, she suddenly felt utterly drained and exhausted. She realized she hadn't had any food since lunch time, but the thought of preparing something was too much of an effort. She hesitated about having more brandy and decided against it. Getting to her feet, she walked slowly into the kitchen and put on the coffee percolator. She sat on a kitchen chair, her head in her hands, her eyes closed and remained like that until the coffee was ready. She sipped the strong black coffee which revived her a little, then as she was putting down the empty cup, she heard a sound that brought her alert.

She sprang to her feet and went to the kitchen door and looked across the hall to the cellar door. As she stood listening, her heart beginning to thump, the sound came again: a low moaning sigh. It was such an uncanny sound that it turned her cold.

Shakily, she crossed the hall and stood close to the cellar door, holding her breath, so tense, her muscles began to ache. The sound came again.

Was Archer having an attack? He had been behaving like an infuriated bull and if he did have a bad heart as he said he had he might have brought on an attack. She cringed at the thought. Suppose he died?

Then very faintly through the door panel as if he were crouched against the other side of the door, she heard him murmur, 'Helga? Helga?'

'What is it?' Her voice quavering and husky.

'It's my heart.' He made a low whimpering sound. 'There are tablets in my overcoat pocket. Get them . . . quickly.'

She looked at the black overcoat lying on the hall chair. With shaking hands she searched the pocket and her fingers closed around a glass phial. She took it out and stared at it. It contained about eight oval shaped tablets. There was no label attached to the phial.

The moan came again.

Without thinking, now in a blind panic, she caught hold of the pole to jerk it free, but it was jammed so tight, she couldn't move it.

'For God's sake, Helga . . . I'm dying,' Archer called. 'Give me those tablets!'

The harsh note in his voice tinged with angry impatience made her pause. Was he bluffing? She looked at the phial. These could be anything: digestive tablets, sleeping pills . . . anything.

'Helga? Are you there?' His voice was stronger as if he was afraid she might have moved away and wouldn't hear him.

If he was bluffing and she opened the door, she would be at his mercy, she thought. But suppose he wasn't? Suppose he really was having a heart attack?

She moved to the door.

'They're not there. Would they be in the car?'

'They're there!' There was now a snarl in his voice. 'You haven't looked! A phial with white tablets in it. Look again! Open the door . . . I can't breathe! For God's sake, Helga, don't let me die!'

The snarl in his voice stiffened her resolve not to open the door. Moving unsteadily, she went into the sitting-room and closed the door. She crossed to the bar and poured brandy into a glass and swallowed it in one shuddering gulp. Then she dropped on to the settee.

If he died . . . he died! She dare not risk opening the cellar door. He had shown no mercy to her. Why should she show mercy to him? A blackmailer is the dirtiest thing on earth. Let him die! She would be free of him then forever! But she knew she was desperately trying to justify her action. She knew that it was only because she was exerting tremendous control over herself she wasn't rushing to his aid.

He's bluffing, she tried to assure herself. He's un-scrupulous, ruthless and an expert bluffer. She held her head in her hands. But was he bluffing?

Suppose, when Larry returned, they found Archer dead? The thought sickened her. What would they do? How would Larry react? She touched her dry lips with her tongue. If he died she would have to call a doctor. Would the news of his death travel fast? Would the Bank hear of it before they posted the letter? *In the event of my death!* They certainly wouldn't post the letter to a dead man. They would act on his instructions and get a messenger to hand the envelope to Herman when he arrived at Geneva.

She struck her clenched fists together in an agony of indecision and despair. Getting to her feet, she opened the sitting-room door to listen.

Faintly, she could hear a sound on the lower panel of the cellar door. Irregular sounds, as if feeble fingernails were tapping on the panel.

'Helga ... the tablets ...' Archer's voice was now so faint she could scarcely hear it. 'The tablets.'

With her hands pressed to her ears, Helga blundered into her bedroom and threw herself face down on the bed.

The sound of the garage doors slamming shut startled her out of a sleep of exhaustion. Dazed, she scrambled off the bed. She was so unsteady she had to sit down abruptly on the bed or she would have fallen. She looked at her watch. The time was 03.10.

Had Larry returned?

She forced herself to her feet and stumbled out of the bedroom and into the hall. She looked fearfully at the cellar door, and then she went to the front door and opened it.

By the porch light, she saw it was snowing heavily and the cold struck at her. She saw Larry coming towards her, holding the envelope she had given him.

It was only the steel in her that prevented her from bursting into tears of relief.

He came up the steps, chewing hard and smiling his warm smile.

'I got it, ma'am! Get inside and ... you'll catch cold.'

She stepped back, her knees trembling and she had to clutch hold of the door to prevent herself falling. He gave her a searching stare and then caught hold of her, pushing the front door shut.

'Are you all right, ma'am?'

'I'm so glad you're back.' Her voice broke and then the

126

tears came and she leaned against him, shaking and sobbing.

'Hey, ma'am! What's the matter? Did you . . .' He stopped as he saw the pole jamming the cellar door. 'Did you have trouble?'

'Oh, God . . . yes!'

He lifted her off her feet and carried her into the sitting-room. Gently, he put her on the settee.

'What happened, ma'am? He didn't get away?'

She fought to control herself and succeeded. As she dabbed her eyes with her handkerchief, she said, 'No . . . but, Larry . . . I – I think he's dead.'

Larry took a step back. His look of concern changed to wide-eyed fright.

'Dead?'

She nodded.

'I nearly went out of my mind!' She beat her fists together. 'He said he was having a heart attack.' She had to stop speaking to fight back her tears, then after a moment, she went on, 'It was awful! He was moaning and calling to me! He wanted some tablets. I was too frightened to open the door to give them to him. Then he started knocking . . . and now . . . there's no sound . . . nothing.' She shuddered, her face working. 'I'm so frightened. I didn't know if he was bluffing. I couldn't let him out . . . could I?'

Larry stared at her. His face had turned chalk white and his eyes turned remote. After a long silence, he said huskily. 'But you don't know he is really dead?'

'No. Please go and see.'

He flinched and retreated further away from her.

'What will you do if he is dead?' he asked.

'I don't know. I haven't thought. For God's sake, Larry, go and see!'

He retreated further away from her.

'I – I don't like anything to do with dead people. No . . . I don't want to do that.'

She understood and didn't blame him. After all, she told herself he was only an immature boy.

'We must know! I'll go, but come with me, Larry. He may be bluffing and he might attack me. Will you come with me?'

Larry hesitated, then nodded.

'Sure, ma'am. I'll come with you.'

Shaking, Helga went into the hall.

'I can't move that.' She indicated the pole. 'Will you try?'

Larry took hold of the pole in his huge hands, twisted and gave it a jerk. It came free. He laid it down along the wall, then catching hold of the chest, he dragged it away from the door which swung open.

Helga saw the lights were on in the corridor below. She moved to the head of the stairs and stood listening. She could only hear the steady roar of the motor, driving the central heating. Gathering her courage, she began to descend the stairs. Halfway down, she paused and looked back. Larry was standing at the top of the stairs, his face shiny with sweat. They looked at each other.

'Come with me,' she whispered.

He nodded and came down the stairs, then stopped. She went on and paused when she was in the corridor.

'Jack?' Her voice was so husky it was almost soundless. 'Jack! Are you there?'

The silence that greeted her gripped her with a paralysing terror. She couldn't bring herself to move forward. She remained motionless, staring down the long corridor at the shattered cellar door at the far end of the corridor and opposite, the games room: the door stood ajar. The other doors leading to the boiler room and to two more cellars were closed.

He must be dead, she thought hopelessly. He must be lying in the cellar. He must have crawled there. She fought off the terror that gripped her and the steel in her that never failed her stiffened her courage.

'Come with me!' she said, her voice hardening. 'Larry! You're in this as much as I am!'

Hesitating, Larry came down three more of the stairs and then stopped.

She went along the corridor, paused, then forced herself to look into the cellar. Except for the splinters of wood on the concrete floor, the cellar was empty. She turned and looked at the door, standing ajar, leading to the games room. She could see the room was in darkness. She saw Larry hadn't moved. He was standing halfway down the stairs, sweat trickling down his face. She felt a sudden contempt for him. His fear increased her courage. She walked to the games room, threw the door open, groped for the light switch and turned it on.

With her heart hammering, she looked around the big room. There was no sign of Archer.

He couldn't have escaped!

To convince herself she looked at the steel door at the far end of the corridor, leading to the garage. She could see from where she stood that the bolt of the lock was home.

There was another cellar and the boiler room in which Archer could be hiding or lying dead. She went to the boiler room and threw the door open. The door was near the bottom of the stairs, and as she turned on the light, Larry retreated up two stairs. She looked around. Again there was no sign of Archer. She was shaking again, and she turned to look at Larry.

Pointing to the second cellar door, she mouthed without speaking, 'He's in there . . . the other is locked.'

Looking scared, Larry stared blankly at her. Her silent mouthing conveyed nothing to him. She motioned him to come down into the corridor and reluctantly he did so. The unlocked cellar door opened outwards. She put a shaking hand on the door handle, turned it and flung the door open.

Archer came out like a charging bull. Helga was standing back, but Larry was directly in his path. Archer's fist, thrust forward like a battering ram, thudded into Larry's chest, with all Archer's heavy weight behind it, sending him reeling. Larry tried to regain his balance as Archer rushed by him, but he went sprawling.

'Larry!' Helga screamed.

Archer stumbled on the stairs and fell on his knees. He was so heavy and cumbersome he took a long moment to get to his feet. By then Larry was up and he grabbed hold of Archer's left ankle. Archer kicked back wildly with his right foot which whistled by Larry's face. Larry hauled him back down the stairs.

Cursing, Archer broke free and rolled over. Lying on his back, panting, he glared helplessly up at Larry.

As Larry got set to kick him, Helga screamed, 'Don't touch him!'

Scowling, Larry stepped back and wiped his sweating face with the back of his hand.

Lying still, Archer looked up at Helga, his face a blotchy white.

'So you've got your pimp back,' he said huskily. 'All right ... you win. Just leave me alone.'

She felt a moment of pity. The bruise on the side of his face had extended and was now blue and yellow. His lips were swollen and dried blood caked on his chin. He looked old, frightened and defeated.

'I warned you, Jack,' she said shakily. 'I'm sorry.'

'I imagine.' His voice was bitter. Slowly he crawled to his feet and leaned against the wall. 'Sorry? You wouldn't know the meaning of the word.'

She pointed to the games room.

'You'll be comfortable in there. I'll get you a drink.'

He lurched by Larry who was tense, his huge hands on his hips, his jaw moving as he chewed. Then Archer passed Helga and went into the games room.

Helga went unsteadily up the stairs to the sitting-room. She mixed a double whisky and soda, added ice and carried the drink down to the games room.

Archer was sitting in one of the lounging chairs, his head in his hands. She put the drink on the covered billiard table.

'Do you want something to eat?'

'Oh, go to hell!' he said wearily and without viciousness. 'Leave me alone.'

She went out and closed the door. Motioning Larry to follow her, she climbed the stairs.

'Put the pole back, Larry,' she said and went into the sitting-room. With shaking hands she opened the envelope Larry had brought back and took out the three sheets of paper, stripped off two and looked at the letter. The signature was a replica of Archer's scrawl. She found one of Archer's letters and compared the two signatures, then she drew in a shaky breath of relief. She was sure the Bank would accept the forgery.

'Is it okay, ma'am?' Larry asked as he came into the room.

'Yes, I think so. Did he ask questions?'

Larry shook his head.

'He wanted five thousand but I beat him down to three five. I spent money on gas, but I have some change for you.'

'Don't bother me with that!' she said impatiently. She went to her desk and typed an envelope. 'I'm going down to Lugano to mail this. If you're hungry there's food on the table in the kitchen. It should be defrosted by now.'

'I'll mail it, ma'am. The roads are bad and it's snowing hard.'

'No! I won't stay here alone. I'm going.'

'Be careful, ma'am. The roads are real mean.'

She went into the hall and put on her coat. He followed her and stood lolling against the wall, chewing, and watching her.

'Don't go to sleep until I get back,' she said. 'Eat something.' She looked at the pole jammed against the cellar door. 'He can't get out, can he?'

Larry grinned.

'With me around, ma'am, he won't try.'

She put on her hat and looked at herself in the hall mirror. God! she thought, how old I look!

She put the letter in her bag. She found a pair of fur-lined boots in the recess and put them on.

'I won't be long.'

'Okay, ma'am ... if you're sure you want to go.'

She opened the front door and shivered as the cold bit at her. She cautiously made her way down the snow-covered steps. On the fourth step she nearly slipped but recovered.

'Watch it, ma'am!' Larry said from the opened doorway.

She kept on and reached the garage. Once inside the warm car she relaxed a little. She knew the road down to Lugano well. She knew the three danger points. She set the car in motion. The snow tyres bit into the snow and she drove cautiously.

She met no other car nor any other person. Three times the car went into a skid, but she was an experienced driver and although she hated skids, she controlled the car.

Eventually, after some fifteen minutes of difficult driving, she reached the Central Post Office. She parked the car, got out and dropped the letter into the box.

With the snow falling heavily, making her coat into a white mantle, she stood for a moment, relaxing.

The first step in the operation was completed. Now it remained to be seen if the Bank would send the envelope. Shaking the snow off her coat, she went back to the car and got in. She lit a cigarette, staring through the windshield while she thought. The time by the lighted clock on the dashboard was 03.55. She realized how deadly tired she was. She thought with dread of the thirty odd hours ahead of her before she could expect a reply from the bank. If this snow continued, there would be no question of Herman surprising her. He took too good care of himself to fly when the weather was bad.

She shifted the lever to *Drive* and drove back towards Castagnola. Driving around the steep climbing bend into the village, the Mercedes got out of control. The back wheels skidded and the car turned broadside on across the road and then began to slide sideways down the hill. She spun the driving wheel, touched the gas pedal and got the bonnet of the car pointing up hill again, but the hill was too steep for a take-off and the wheels merely spun, moving the rear of the car until the wheels thudded against the kerb. She sat motionless for some moments wondering what to do. Finally she decided she must make a new attack on the hill. She went into reverse and backed slowly down the hill until she reached the entrance to Cassarate which was on the level. She paused, fighting her tiredness, then drawing on her reserve stamina, she again started up the hill. This time she kept her foot very lightly on the gas pedal, but just enough to keep the engine going. In this way, with the snow tyres biting, the car crawled up the hill.

She realized there was no question of her getting the car up the private road to the villa. When the entrance was in sight, she pulled the car to the side of the road and got out.

Leaving the parking lights on, she slipped and slid up the drive, until she finally reached the front door of the villa. She was cold, stunned and exhausted as she pressed the door bell.

After a brief delay, Larry opened the door.

'You made it, ma'am?'

Wearily, she took off her coat and thrust it into his hands.

'Shake it. Don't bring all that snow into the house.'

She sank on to the chest, closing her eyes. The warmth that seeped through her was comforting.

'It's mean out there, isn't it?' he said as he shut the door.

'Yes . . . I had to leave the car in the road.'

She took off her hat and let it drop on the floor.

'Food's ready, ma'am. Come on and eat.'

She shook her head.

'No. I couldn't. I'm going to bed. I must sleep.' Her voice broke. 'I'm so tired.' She pressed her palms to her eyes. 'Your room is at the end of the corridor, Larry.' She could smell the fillet of pork and the onions cooking. The smell made her cringe.

She got wearily to her feet and walked towards her bedroom, then she paused and looked back.

'Is he all right?' She pressed the back of her hand against her forehead. 'Shouldn't you give him something to eat?'

'You go to bed, ma'am. There's nothing for you to worry about,' Larry said gently. 'I'll take care of him.'

She was too tired to care.

'Good night, Larry . . . and thank you.'

His warm smile gave her renewed confidence.

'You sleep, ma'am . . . you'll be fine tomorrow.'

She nodded.

'It's going to be all right, Larry.'

'Sure.'

She went along to her bedroom and closed the door. Slowly, she undressed. Her movements were listless. She put on her pyjamas, then too tired even to brush her teeth, she got into bed. She reached up and turned off the light.

Then for the first time in many years, she began to pray, but she was asleep before the prayer was finished.

CHAPTER SEVEN

A GENTLE tapping on the door brought Helga awake with a start. Her mind flashed back to the events of the night and her heart began to hammer. She struggled up in bed.

'Who is it?'

'Me, ma'am. Would you like some coffee?'

She relaxed back on her pillow. Sunlight was coming through the shutters and drapes. She turned on the bedside light and looked at her watch. It was 09.15.

'I'd love some coffee, please.'

'Like something to eat, ma'am?'

She realized she hadn't eaten since lunch-time the previous day and she was hungry.

'An egg, Larry.'

'Okay, ma'am.'

'Give me about fifteen minutes.'

'Sure, ma'am,' and she heard him walk away.

She got out of bed and went into the bathroom. It took her longer than fifteen minutes to fix her face and her hair, but when she had finished and regarded herself in the mirror, she was satisfied. She dressed quickly, pulling on a heavy cable stitch sweater and cavalry twill slacks.

As she left her bedroom, Larry came from the kitchen, carrying a tray.

'All ready, ma'am.'

He followed her into the sitting-room and put the tray on the table. He had cooked her an omelette, browned to a turn and as light as any omelette Hinkle had ever cooked. Toast, marmalade and a big pot of coffee completed the meal.

'You're a real cook, Larry,' she said as she sat down. 'This looks wonderful.'

He grinned, pleased.

'Yeah, I reckon if there's one thing I can do, it's to cook.'

As she flicked open the napkin, she asked. 'Is he all right?'

Larry sat in a lounging chair. He took out a packet of chewing gum.

'Sure. I let him use the bathroom. I gave him a steak for breakfast. He won't be any trouble now. He knows when he's licked.'

She relaxed and began to enjoy her breakfast.

'I was worried about you last night, Larry. The drive must have been horrible. You were wonderfully quick.'

'It was okay, but I wouldn't say I was quick. Coming back was bad.' He shrugged. 'I made it.'

She ate in silence for some minutes, then she asked, 'You didn't leave the man alone with the letter?'

'No, ma'am ... don't worry. I never left him. He didn't like it, but Ron's right. Maxie would cut his own throat for money.'

The omelette finished, she began to butter toast.

'Did you call Ron?' she asked, her voice falsely casual.

'Yeah, I called him.' He leaned forward, his huge hands resting on his knees. 'You see, ma'am, Ron means a lot to me. I wanted him to know I was helping you. After the names he called me, I wanted him to know I was doing my best for you.'

'What did he say?'

'He was pleased.'

Suddenly she didn't want to eat any more. She laid down the toast and pushed aside her plate.

'Did you tell him Archer was here?'

He shook his head.

'No, ma'am ... nothing like that. I just told him I was helping you.'

She reached for a cigarette, relaxing a little.

'You must never speak to anyone about Archer being here, Larry.'

'Sure, ma'am. You don't have to worry.'

But still she wasn't satisfied.

'But didn't Ron want to know how you were helping me?'

He rubbed his mouth with the back of his hand and she could see he was uneasy.

'Yeah, he did ask. I told him we were getting the photos back.'

Her hands turned into fists.

'Did you tell him how . . . about Max?'

He shifted about in his chair, then he said, 'Well, ma'am, I had to. I did tell him Maxie was helping. But that's okay, ma'am, Maxie and Ron are good friends. Ron was pleased Maxie was helping.'

Helga got stiffly to her feet and walked over to an occasional table. She picked up a lighter and lit her cigarette.

'Didn't he ask how Max was helping?'

'No, ma'am . . . he wasn't interested. He had other things on his mind.'

'What things?'

Larry looked blankly at her.

'He didn't tell me, ma'am.'

Helga pressed her hands to her face. Her whole future life was in the hands of these men. This magnificent-looking boy could have been an idiot for all the help she could get from him!

After a long pause, Larry said, 'There's a fat guy out there clearing the snow. As soon as he's through I'll bring up the car.'

Relieved to do something, Helga went to the window. Below she saw her fat road sweeper friend shovelling the snow from the drive. A wheelbarrow full of grit stood nearby.

'I'll bring the car up, Larry,' she said. 'You must keep out of sight. Village people talk. I don't want him to see you.'

'Yeah . . . there's that. Have you finished?'

'Yes . . . thank you. It was beautifully cooked.'

He picked up the tray and took it into the kitchen.

She stood by the window watching the road sweeper and when she saw he was finishing, she went into the bedroom took a fifty franc note from her bag, put on her coat, snow shoes and hat and went down the drive. The road sweeper lifted his cap when he saw her. She spent a few minutes chatting with him. He asked respectfully after her husband. He told her there would be no more snow but she didn't believe him. The village people always told foreigners that better weather was coming. She gave him the fifty franc note and he jerked off his cap, his face wreathed in smiles, then she went down to the car and drove it up to the garage.

She returned to the villa. As she shut the front door, hearing Larry in the kitchen, the telephone bell began to ring. Stripping off her coat and dropping it on the chest, she started for the sitting-room as Larry appeared in the kitchen doorway.

'It's all right,' she said curtly. 'I'll handle it.'

'Sure, ma'am,' and he went back into the kitchen.

She reached the telephone and picked up the receiver.

'Mrs. Rolfe?'

'Yes . . . who is it?'

'A call from New York. Mr. Rolfe. A moment, please.'

She drew in a breath of exasperation, sat down and reached for a cigarette. As she was lighting, Rolfe's querulous voice came on the line.

'Helga?'

'Yes. Did you get my telex?'

'I did . . . what's going on? I called the Eden and they told me you had checked out.'

'My dear man, the only way to get this goddamn villa ready for you is to be here,' Helga said, her voice shrill. 'I'm wearing my fur coat if that interests you and it is bloody cold! Why are you calling?'

'Helga! You don't have to use such language!'

'Don't tempt me, Herman. I'm cold and fed up. I can use a lot worse!'

'I do wish you wouldn't talk like this. Now listen to me, I want you to come back to New York at once. I'm not coming to Castagnola. I have sudden business in the Bahamas. The Eden tells me it is snowing in Lugano. You know I don't like the snow. I've decided to go to Nassau. You'll join me. You'll enjoy the sun. There is a flight from Milan at four o'clock this afternoon to New York. We'll fly together to Nassau tomorrow.'

Helga gripped the telephone receiver so hard her nails turned white.

'That's impossible,' she said. 'I have the cleaning women here and I can't and won't pack in a minute!'

She heard her husband snort.

'Oh, nonsense! You have plenty of time. Now don't start making difficulties.'

'I intend to make difficulties! I have things to do here. Besides, it is snowing and I'm not driving to Milan in this goddamn snowstorm just to please your whim! If you can't wait for me, then go ahead and I'll join you at the end of the week. Where will you be staying?'

'I don't see why you should get so worked up,' Herman complained. 'I insist you moderate your language when you talk to me.'

'Where will you be staying?' Helga said, raising her voice.

'The Emerald Beach hotel for two days, then I hope Hinkle will find us a furnished bungalow.' Herman's voice had turned sulky. 'I don't see why you can't come at once. You're always making difficulties, Helga.'

She wanted to scream at him to go to hell, but she bit that back.

'That's a charming remark, Herman, considering I have been freezing in this damned place so you could arrive in comfort!'

She heard him snort impatiently.

'I don't see why you should even be there. You just don't know how to get things organized.'

'I'll fly to New York on Saturday and not before!'

'I'm not going to wait for you. I'm leaving for Nassau tomorrow morning.'

'I'll join you when I'm ready.' She paused, took hold of herself and softening her voice, she asked, 'How are you?'

They spent a few more minutes talking indifferently to each other, then she hung up.

Well, at least now, she wouldn't have to worry about Herman and that was a relief.

The sun was shining and the countryside from the picture window looked clean, white and sparkling.

She went into the kitchen where Larry was finishing the washing-up.

'You don't have to do that. There's a dishwasher.'

'Yeah ... I see that, but it foxes me. I've never used one.'

Helga realized she had never used a dishwasher either and she laughed. 'There's a book of instructions somewhere.'

'I don't mind doing the washing-up,' Larry said. 'That's all I did in the Army.'

Then she remembered what Archer had said: that Larry was an Army deserter.

'You were in the Army?'

He looked at her, his face expressionless.

'You know that, ma'am ... Archer told you.'

She nodded.

'He told me you are a deserter.'

'That's it ... AWOL. That's me.' He dried his hands and leaned against the double sink. 'I had enough of the Army so I walked out.'

She studied him, then she hoisted herself on the kitchen table, swinging her shapely legs.

'So all that talk about your father sending you to Europe was so much talk?'

He ran his fingers through his blond hair.

'Excuse me, ma'am. I didn't mean to snow you, but you asked and I guess I said the first thing that came into my head.'

'That's all right, Larry. I understand.'

'Thank you, ma'am.'

'So your position is more difficult than I thought. If the Army police ...'

'There are no M.P.s here, ma'am. I'm not worrying.'

No, she thought, you may not be worrying, but I am.

'I intend to fly back to New York on Saturday,' she said. 'What will you do when I've gone?'

'Saturday?' This seemed to give him a jolt. He frowned as he thought. 'I'll manage. I'll get a job at a hotel or at a filling station ... something like that.'

'We've gone over that before, Larry. You need a work permit.'

'Yeah.' He rubbed the back of his head and his frown deepened. 'Well, don't you worry, ma'am. I'll manage somehow.'

'But how?'

He looked up and his frown went away. He gave her his warm, friendly smile.

'I don't know right now. I'll have to think about it, but as Ron said: a problem is a challenge and I guess this is my problem.'

'I'd like to help you. You've helped me. Would you like to go home?'

He stared at her.

'I sure would, ma'am, but I can't. That's the first place the cops would look for me. No . . . I can't go home.'

'But you would like to go back to the States?'

'Yeah . . . I guess I would.'

'If I gave you your ticket and some money, Larry, would you be able to get a job?'

He nodded.

'Sure . . . I've got this faked passport. I could easily get a job if I went back.'

'All right, Larry, then that's what I'll do. When the bank sends the photos, I'll book a seat for you on the New York flight and I'll give you a present of five thousand dollars. Would that be all right?'

He stared as if he couldn't believe what he was hearing, then his face lit up: the face of a child who has seen Father Christmas for the first time.

'Do you really mean that, ma'am?'

'Yes . . . I mean it. I owe you a lot, Larry.'

He thought, then shook his head.

'No, ma'am. I wouldn't say that. I got you into this mess.'

She was glad he said that.

'That's honest of you, Larry. Yes, you did get me into this mess.' She lifted her hands and let them drop into her lap. 'But to be as honest as you, I admit I was heading for a mess anyway, and I'm lucky it was with you and not with some other man without scruples.' She smiled at him as she slid off the table. 'Now I'm going down to the village. I feel like a walk. I'll get some fresh bread. Is there anything you want?'

'I'm getting short of gum ... if I could bother you.'

'I'll get you some. You must keep out of sight. Will you be very bored?'

He grinned.

'Bored? No, ma'am, I don't get bored. I'll get you a good lunch.'

She smiled.

'Wonderful! I won't be more than an hour or so.' She went into the hall and put on her coat. Larry came to the kitchen door. 'If anyone comes ... if the telephone rings ... don't answer.'

'Sure, ma'am ... I know.' He paused, then went on, 'When do you think the bank will send the photos?'

'Not until the day after tomorrow.'

'You think they will send them?'

She nodded.

'Yes ... the signature is convincing.'

'Yeah, I guess Maxie is smart.'

Smiling, she put her hand on his arm.

'I don't know what I would have done without you, Larry.'

She opened the front door and feeling suddenly young and almost happy, she hurried out into the sunshine and the cold.

The walk to the village with the cold nipping at her invigorated her. Her problems, she told herself, were slowly coming under control. Herman was out of the way. Archer was locked up. She would give Larry five thousand dollars and his ticket to New York and her debt to him would be paid. When she saw Herman she would tell him about the missing two million dollars, blaming herself as much as Archer, but insisting the account should be transferred to Spencer, Grove & Manly. She would be able to fly to New York with a completely free mind. Then Nassau! Yes, she felt in need of warm sunshine and the sea, and from now on, she told herself, no more men!

She bought bread, and after some trouble, four packs of

chewing gum. She was in an almost gay mood as she walked up the road, back to the villa.

It was 11.50 by the time she reached the front door. She took her key from her bag and opened the door, pleased to come into the warm.

'Larry?'

She took off her coat. She wished the scaffolding pole hadn't to remain, jamming the cellar door. She disliked untidiness, and the pole spoilt the neatness of the hall.

'Larry?'

The silence that greeted her made her pause to listen. Hearing nothing, she took off her hat and went into the kitchen. There was a chicken in its plastic wrapping defrosting on the table, a packet of spinach and a packet of dehydrated potatoes, but no Larry.

Suddenly alarmed, she went to the sitting-room and threw open the door.

Facing her, sitting in a lounging chair, a whisky and soda in his hand, was Archer.

The shock of seeing him sent the blood from her face.

'Did you have a nice walk?' Archer asked mildly.

Helga's hands turned into fists. She tried to speak but no sound came.

'A bit of a shock? Of course ... let me get you a drink.' He heaved himself to his feet and moved to the bar. 'The usual?'

'Where's Larry?' Her voice was a croaking whisper.

'Ah, Larry ... Larry is downstairs. He's a little under the weather, but he's all right.' Archer rattled ice cubes in the cocktail shaker. 'After all, he's young and tough. Sit down Helga.'

She stood motionless, her brain scarcely working as she watched him make the cocktail, pour it with a flourish and bring the glass to an occasional table.

'Sit down ... sit down, Helga. I'm afraid you'll have to cook the lunch.' He regarded her. 'I hope you can cook ... I can't.' He sank into his chair and picked up his glass.

'What have you done to him? What happened?' Helga remained motionless. She now had control of herself and was desperately trying to absorb the shock.

'It was really rather simple.' Archer sipped his drink, then took his cigar case from his pocket and selected a cigar. 'Larry isn't over bright. You have probably noticed that. I was listening at the door and I heard your conversation. When you had gone, I called to him. I asked for a cup of coffee. He's young, and the young have too much confidence. He hasn't ever taken me seriously ... his mistake. He brought me a cup of coffee. I hid in the boiler room and as he went to the games room, I sneaked up behind him and hit him on the head with a billiard cue. So easy, Helga, it was almost ridiculous. I came up here, put your ingenious pole in place and that's that.'

Slowly, she moved forward and sat down. Her mind refused to work.

'Have you hurt him?'

He touched the side of his bruised face gently.

'No more than he hurt me.'

'I want to go down and see him. You might have injured him seriously.'

'You're not going, so shut up!' His voice turned vicious. 'I've had about enough of you! He's all right. I just stunned him. He was trying to get to his feet when I reached the hall.' He lit his cigar, then went on, 'You have the three aces now, Helga ... I have the four.'

She was shaking so badly that she had to keep her hands gripped between her knees.'

'I see now, Helga, you're damned dangerous,' he went on. 'I suppose I gave you the idea to forge my signature. Well, tit for tat. So the pansy made a good job of it?'

Helga said nothing.

'Well, my next move is to telephone the bank and tell them to ignore the letter.' Archer got to his feet. 'Then we are back on square A.'

'Wait!'

The snap in her voice made him pause and regard her thoughtfully.

'What little trickery is now going on in your mind?'

'I don't intend to be blackmailed! I have had time to think and I have thought. My life with Herman is getting more and more deadly.' Helga had control of herself. This was the time to bluff, but it would have to be expert bluff. 'Rather than submit to blackmail, I'm prepared to give up my inheritance.'

'How dramatic! The dialogue is right out of a Victorian novel,' Archer said and smiled. 'Not you, Helga. That's something I'll never believe.'

She shrugged.

'I couldn't care less what you believe or don't believe. I mean it. I intend to have those photographs. If I don't get them, then I'm going to call the police and I will charge you with embezzlement. Go ahead and call your bank ... then I'll call the police.'

'Oh come! It's nice bluff but it won't work with me,' Archer said but he didn't move to the telephone.

'Then I'll call the police and after, you call the bank.'

She got up and went to the telephone. She picked up the receiver and began to dial.

He came blundering over and snatched the receiver from her hand.

'Don't be so hasty, Helga.' She saw the uneasiness in his eyes. 'You haven't touched your drink. Let's sit down like civilized people and discuss this.'

She realized she had won the first move in the game. She had frightened him. Her face expressionless, she went back to her chair and sat down. She was pleased that when she picked up her drink, her hand was steady. She sipped and nodded.

'Your martinis are always good.'

He lowered his bulk into his chair.

'Thank you.' He studied the end of his cigar. 'Suppose I let you have the photographs ... what will be your contribution?'

'I will tell Herman we both speculated and lost and the account must be taken from you.'

He shook his head.

'No. That's back to square A. Let's move to square B. You take all the blame for the gamble and I keep the account.'

It was her turn to shake her head.

'No, Jack. You're through. The only other alternative is you go to jail.'

'And you lose sixty million dollars?'

'Yes, but I'm prepared to do just that, but are you prepared to spend ten years in jail? What are you now . . . forty-eight? No one will want an ex-jailbird at fifty-eight, will they?'

She watched him lick his lips.

'You're very persuasive, Helga,' he said finally, 'but I simply don't believe you. You were always a good bluffer but you're not bluffing me.'

'Then call the bank, Jack, and I'll call the police . . . it's as simple as that.'

'Suppose we move to square C?' Archer said, studying the end of his cigar. 'I told you: without Herman's account I am in financial trouble. I owe money everywhere and I'm being pressed. I would like to go back to the States. I could make a fresh start. Now suppose I give you the photographs and give up the account and in return you give me a substantial sum of money so I can clear my debts and make a fresh start back home? What do you say?'

'I will not submit to blackmail,' Helga said quietly.

'You could afford two hundred and fifty thousand dollars, Helga. For that sum you get the photographs and the negatives and eventually you'll collect sixty million dollars. Come on, Helga, that's a fair bargain.'

She reached for a cigarette and lit it, then she sipped her drink.

'And where do you imagine I'd find two hundred and fifty thousand dollars?'

'Any Swiss bank would lend you that against Herman's securities. He needn't know.'

She shook her head.

'You have made a mistake, Jack. You should never have picked on me to blackmail. I'm not the blackmailing type. This morning as I lay in bed, I thought about my possible future. I discovered I am utterly bored and sick of Herman. I want my freedom. I want to be able to take a lover when I need one. I thought about all the money. Sixty million? It's too much. I wouldn't know what to do with such an enormous sum. Then I worked out what I would be worth if Herman divorced me and I was pleasantly surprised. I find I wouldn't be badly off if he threw me out.' She was lying steadily and she hoped convincingly. 'There are things you don't know. For instance you don't know that Herman gave me for my last birthday bonds that will bring me in an income of ten thousand dollars a year. (A lie.) He gave me for my birthday before last a cottage in Carmel where I could live very happily and comfortably. (Another lie.) I have two hundred thousand dollars worth of jewellery. (True.) I have five fur coats: all valuable. (Also true.) I have a car and a motor cruiser. (Again true.) Herman also gave me a Picasso which is worth at least a hundred thousand. (A lie there was no Picasso.) If I sell carefully and invest carefully, I will have an assured income of thirty thousand dollars for life, plus a cottage. (God! she thought, how I wish all this was true!) So I have come to the conclusion that it might be good to be rid of Herman so the answer to square C as you put it, is no.'

He stared at her for a long moment and she met his eyes without flinching.

'Do you really mean that, Helga? You're not bluffing?'

'No, I'm not bluffing.' She finished her drink. 'I think I would like another, please.'

His set face relaxed a little.

'Let's both have another.'

He went over to the bar.

'You see, Helga,' he said as he mixed the cocktail, 'if you really mean all you've been saying, then I'll be forced to move to square D. I don't want to do that, but if you're not bluffing, then I'll have to.'

The tone of his voice and the expression on his fat face made Helga alert.

'And what is square D?' she asked.

'I will sell the photograph of you showing everything you've got to Herman.'

She kept the expression of her face deadpan with an effort.

'And do you imagine he will buy it?'

'Yes, I think he would if I threatened, unless he did, I'll send it to the pornographers. As a dirty postcard it would have a very wide sale.'

Inwardly she flinched.

'And in the meantime you would be in jail?'

'I don't think so. I have also been doing some thinking. I have an idea that Herman wouldn't prosecute if I convinced him that on a dirty postcard his wife would be quite a star attraction.'

She forced herself to brazen it out.

'Then you don't know Herman. He would divorce me and not only prosecute you for embezzling but also for blackmail. You could go to jail for twenty years.'

Archer shrugged.

'Desperate situations need desperate measures. I think Herman would play. The last thing he would want would be to know his cronies were sniggering over your pretty nakedness.'

There came a sudden thudding sound from the hall that brought Archer to his feet. Helga also stood up.

Then Archer smiled.

'Your pimp trying to break out,' he said and sat down again. 'That's something he won't do. That pole was a bright idea of yours, Helga. It is strong enough to pen in a bull. I know . . . I've tried.'

Still standing, she stubbed out her cigarette. Her mind was working swiftly. She knew she was caught unless she could find another way out. She was sure Herman would pay rather than let the photograph go into circulation. Archer would get his money and his freedom and she would lose everything! Her bluff had failed!

'Are you all right, ma'am?' Larry bawled through the door.

'Don't move, Helga,' Archer said, stretching out his long, thick legs. 'Never mind about him. Sit down. What do you think of square D?'

She picked up her drink.

'Ma'am!' Larry's voice crashed into the room.

She braced herself, then taking a quick step forward she threw the contents of her glass in Archer's face. Spinning around, she darted into the hall. She threw herself against the pole. It shuddered but held. She heard a roar of rage from Archer and as she heaved frantically at the pole, he came blundering out. The vodka was stinging his eyes and he was half blind. She dodged around the pole, caught hold of it and pulled with all her strength. She felt it shift as Archer struck at her. His fist thudded into her shoulder, sending her staggering back, but somehow, she kept her grip on the pole. It came with her. She sprawled on the floor, the pole on top of her.

The door crashed open and Larry charged out. Archer was frantically wiping his eyes clear with his handkerchief. Larry went for him. The two men crashed together: Archer's fingers at Larry's face and Larry's great fists smashing into Archer's body.

Helga threw the pole from her and she scrambled to her feet. She could hear Archer's sobbing gasps and saw his knees sagging as Larry's fists, moving like pistons, thudded into Archer's fat body.

Archer's legs sagged and he went down on his knees. Larry stepped back, then hit Archer on the side of his jaw. Helga flinched and shut her eyes. To her, it was a terrible blow: a blow that could kill.

When she looked again, Archer was flat on his back, unconscious. His chest was heaving and blood trickled down his nostrils. The skin along his jaw had split and was bleeding.

'No more!' Helga cried. 'Don't . . . don't . . . !'

Muttering to himself, Larry caught hold of Archer's ankles and dragged him to the cellar doorway. Then walking backwards down the stairs, he dragged Archer after him. The sound of Archer's head thumping on each stair made Helga feel faint. She went limply into the sitting-room and flopped on the settee. She lay there with her hands to her face, fighting off the feeling of faintness that threatened her.

Time ceased to exist. She felt she was floating between consciousness and unconsciousness. Then she felt a hand touch her gently.

'Are you all right, ma'am?'

She took her hands from her face. Larry was bending over her, concern and worry in his eyes.

'Yes.' She looked helplessly up at him. 'Did he hurt you?'

'It's okay. I asked for it. You stay right there, ma'am. I'll get you a cup of tea.'

'I don't want anything. Is he all right?'

Larry fingered the back of his head.

'Oh, sure. I wouldn't have believed it. I didn't think he would have had the guts. He didn't telephone the bank?'

'No.'

'I was scared he would do that.'

'I stopped him.'

His warm, friendly smile was comforting.

'Well, you've got guts, ma'am. I thought he'd really fixed us.'

'I did, too.'

He straightened.

'I guess all that excitement has made me hungry. I'll get lunch. Some food will do you good.'

'No! I'll lie on my bed. I just want to stay quiet. You go ahead, Larry.'

His look of concern returned.

'You're feeling bad, ma'am?'

Her face worked as she tried to control her tears. She nodded. He bent and scooped her up effortlessly and carried her into her bedroom. The feel of his hands around her waist and thighs started her blood moving hotly through her body. She relaxed against him. The faint smell of his body sweat, the hardness of his chest against her face, his thorough maleness sent sensuous waves of desire through her. He lowered her on to the bed and gently took off her shoes.

'You rest, ma'am,' he said and going to the window, he pulled the drapes, shutting out the sunshine. 'You just take it easy.'

'You're a wonderful comfort to me, Larry,' she said, watching him as he moved to the door. 'Thank you.'

'He smiled.

'You take it easy.'

He left the room, closing the door after him.

She lay still, wishing he hadn't gone. She now wanted him with a sexual ache that tormented her. She could hear him in the kitchen, whistling softly as he began to prepare a meal for himself. She wanted to call to him. She wanted him to strip off her clothes and take her with this sudden gentleness he had revealed and which she hadn't believed possible in him.

But she didn't call him.

She lay in the semi-darkness, shivering a little. She felt drained and exhausted. She thought of the hours ahead of her before the photographs arrived.

She had to be patient, she told herself and closed her eyes. She gave herself up to the long wait.

When the Grandfather clock in the hall chimed seven, she roused herself. She felt rested and in control of herself. She got off the bed, stripped off her sweater and slacks and then went into the bathroom.

She could hear the television going in the sitting-room.

Her shoulder ached where Archer had hit her and when she looked at herself in the bathroom mirror, she grimaced. There was a black, spreading bruise from her shoulder to her breast. Lifting her eyes to her face, reflected in the mirror, she saw how tired, white and gaunt she looked.

She drew a bath and lay in the comforting hot water for more than half an hour. As she was drying herself, she heard the television set being turned off, then a tapping on her bedroom door.

'Do you feel like something to eat, ma'am?' Larry called.

'Anything . . . something light.'

'Okay, ma'am . . . I'll fix it.'

She worked on her face, spent ten minutes fixing her hair, then she returned to the bedroom. She put on fresh pants, bra and stockings. She stood before her open wardrobe and surveyed the many dresses, costumes and suits. Finally, she selected a simple white silk dress and slipped it on. She put a gold chain around her slim waist and surveyed herself.

Not bad, she thought: tired, but interestingly tired and no longer looking like a hag.

She left her bedroom and went into the sitting-room. She could hear Larry in the kitchen, but she now badly wanted a drink. She made a stiff vodka and martini, then lighting a cigarette and carrying her drink, she went into the kitchen.

Larry was standing by the glowing grill. His jaw was

moving as he chewed. At her entrance, he turned around and his eyes widened a little at the sight of her.

'Gee, ma'am . . . you look beautiful!'

She couldn't remember when a man had said that to her: a long time ago, she thought and she smiled.

'Thank you, Larry. Won't you have a drink?'

'No, thank you, ma'am. Drink doesn't get along with me. I got drunk once and I got into a lot of trouble so I keep away from it.'

'You're wise. What are you cooking?'

'You said you wanted something light. I dug out a couple of soles. I guess this freezer has all the food in the world.'

'I think it has. A sole sounds wonderful.'

She sat on a kitchen chair and sipped her drink.

'Is he all right?' she asked.

'Yeah, I guess. I went down to take a look at him. He's not all that happy. I guess I dug a few into him he didn't like.' Larry pulled the tray from under the grill and expertly turned the soles, then pushed the tray back. 'He's sorry for himself.'

'Perhaps I'd better go down and see him,' Helga said, suddenly worried.

'I wouldn't do that, ma'am. He'll be all right. I made him some soup. You don't have to bother about him.'

'Are you sure he's all right?'

'Yeah . . . he'll survive.'

His indifference alarmed her.

'I'd better see him.'

'No, ma'am. You keep away from him. He's in a nasty mood. There's no point in you seeing him. He'll only call you names.' Larry grinned. 'He called me plenty . . . but tomorrow, he'll be fine.'

She decided to take his advice.

'What have you been doing with yourself all this time?'

'Oh, taking it easy. There was a good football match on the telly.'

'I must have slept. No one telephoned or called?'

'No, ma'am.' He peered into the grill. 'If you feel like it, we can eat.'

She watched while he quickly laid the kitchen table and

then served the soles. She was astonished by his quick efficiency and suddenly ashamed of her own inadequacy. She had no idea how to prepare any meal except a hamburger or possibly to fry an egg which she generally broke when serving it. She realized, as he deftly filleted the soles, how badly she had eaten when she had been without much money: sandwiches, hamburgers and meals from a slot machine.

'I should be doing this, Larry,' she said as he set her plate before her. 'That's what a woman is supposed to do.'

'I guess lots of girls don't know how to cook,' he said and sat down. 'But they can do other things.'

Again she felt hot blood move through her.

'Yes . . . that's right.'

They ate in silence. When they had finished, she said, 'It was wonderful, Larry . . . you really are a great cook.'

'I'm glad it pleased you, ma'am. You take it easy. I'll clear up.' He collected the plates and moved to the sink.

'I must help you.'

He grinned at her.

'I'll manage. You go ahead and take it easy. Coffee?'

'That would be nice.'

She went into the sitting-room, crossed to the bar and poured a small brandy. Then she sat down. As she swirled the brandy around in the balloon glass, she thought of Herman; querulous, selfish, demanding and expecting every attention. This boy was really wonderful! What a marvellous husband he would make for some lucky girl!

She heard him washing up, whistling to himself, then after a while he came in with two cups of coffee.

'Have you given him anything to eat, Larry?' she asked. Archer was preying on her mind. She took the cup of coffee he handed her.

'Don't worry about him, ma'am. He's had soup . . . he's okay.'

'Perhaps I'd better see him. He's not young, Larry, and you hit him terribly hard.'

Larry sat down. He held the cup and saucer awkwardly.

'You leave him alone, ma'am. There's no point in you getting upset. He used some pretty strong language.'

'But you're sure he's all right?'

'Sure . . . sure . . . sure.'

She gave up.

After a pause while they sipped the steaming coffee, she said, 'I'll call the American Express tomorrow and book your seat.'

'Thank you, ma'am.'

She looked at him and smiled.

'I'll miss you, Larry.'

'Yeah . . . I guess I'll miss you, too.'

'It's been a fantastic adventure, hasn't it?'

'It has that.'

Not one of the world's most brilliant conversationalists, she thought with regret, but he is magnificent to look at.

'It's nearly over,' she said. 'The day after tomorrow the photos will come. Then we say goodbye.'

'I guess that's right.'

Watching him, looking at the breadth of his shoulders, his huge hands and his masculinity, she again felt the tormenting sexual urge go through her.

She remembered she had told herself: no more men, but just this once, she thought. We have tonight, all tomorrow and tomorrow night together. She knew she couldn't sit around in the villa, waiting for the hours to pass while she had him with her. Surely, he would feel the same way. She would have to give him a little encouragement: just a hint and he would take her. Tonight: more love during the following day and more love the next night, then she would be satisfied. She would say goodbye and have a memory to live with, and then positively no more men!

'Excuse me, ma'am . . .'

She looked up, jerked away from her thoughts and she smiled at him.

'Yes, Larry?'

'There's an ice hockey match on at nine on the telly. Would it bother you if I watched it?'

She felt as if she had received a slap in the face. She looked down at her hands.

'Of course not . . . if you want to.'

'Yeah . . . I dig for ice hockey. Do you like it ma'am?'

She contained herself with an effort.

'No ... it doesn't interest me.' She looked at the clock on the overmantel. It showed 20.55. 'The programme will be on in five minutes.'

'Yes, ma'am.'

'I'll go to bed. I'll find something to read.'

He went over to the television set and turned it on. She had an idea he hadn't heard what she had said.

She stood up and looked at herself in the wall mirror. Why hadn't she lit a flame in him? she wondered. Ice hockey, for God's sake! She regarded the slim, blonde woman reflected in the glass. She looked pale and perhaps a little tired, but she didn't look anything like her real age. Suppose she went to him and put her arms around him and arched her body hard against his? Would that light the flame? She looked at his broad back as he bent over the set. The announcer was introducing the players as they skated around the rink. He was saying the Swiss side had a hard struggle ahead of them. The Canadian Eagles hadn't been defeated this season.

'Hotdamn!' Larry muttered to himself and sat down before the screen.

She lifted her shoulders helplessly, then she went to the bookcase and took the first book to hand.

The skaters were charging down the rink and she could hear Larry muttering to himself.

She went to the door and opened it.

'I'll read, Larry. I won't be asleep when the game's over. Look in and say goodnight.'

He was leaning forward as three skaters collided and started a punch-up.

'Larry?'

He didn't look around. She was sure he had forgotten her existence. Irritated, she raised her voice, 'Larry!'

He looked over his shoulder, frowning.

'Yes, ma'am?'

'Look in and see me when it's over ... I won't be asleep.'

'Sure ... sure,' and he turned back to the screen.

She went out and into her bedroom.

She stood in the middle of the elegant room, feeling utterly depressed. She supposed she had no sex appeal for him.

She tossed the book on the bed, then began to undress. Going to her closet, she selected a flimsy, see-through nightdress and put it on. Taking the gold clips from her hair, she shook it loose so it cascaded to her shoulders. Then she went into the bathroom. Ten minutes later, she came out and paused to look at herself in the full-length mirror. Surely any man with normal instincts would desire her . . . or was she deceiving herself?

She got into bed, picked up the book and glanced at the title. It was Galsworthy's *Forsyte Saga*. Irene and Soames: a woman's indifference to a man, and with her, the situation was reversed: a man's indifference to a woman. She put the book down. She could hear faintly the exited voice of the commentator, speaking in Italian. She wished Larry would turn off the sound: it was not as if he could understand what the man was saying. She lay back on the pillows and stared up at the ceiling.

Then she heard the telephone bell ring.

Not Herman again? she thought. She was in no mood to listen to his querulous complaints. She picked up the extension receiver by her bed.

'Yes?'

'Is that Mrs. Rolfe?' A harsh male American voice.

She stiffened.

Who on earth could this be? she wondered and said a little hesitantly, 'Yes . . . who is it?'

'You don't know me, but you've heard of me. I'm Smith . . . Ron Smith.'

She sat bolt upright, aware her heart was beginning to thum. What was coming? More blackmail?'

'Do you want to speak to Larry?' she asked.

'Is he there?'

'Yes.'

'Can he hear you?'

'What do you mean?'

'I'm asking you if he is in the same room with you.' There was an important note in the harsh voice now.

'No . . . he's watching television. Do you want to talk to him?'

'I want to talk to you.'

She felt her mouth turn dry. She was sure now he was going to blackmail her.

'I don't think I want to talk to you, Mr. Smith,' she said, trying to keep her voice steady. 'I . . .'

'Cut it out! This is urgent and important to you! I've had a hell of a time getting your phone number. I don't know why I should have bothered. Rich women like you aren't worth bothering about, but a life is a life, even if it is worthless.'

He's mad, she was thinking and she was tempted to replace the receiver, but before she could make up her mind, he went on, 'Mrs. Rolfe, you are in deadly danger. Don't talk . . . listen. I've just got out of jail. I've been locked up for a week. I've been pretty busy but this afternoon I've been going through the newspapers for the past week to check on the political scene.'

'I really can't see what this has to do with me,' Helga said sharply. 'What do you mean . . . deadly danger?'

'Stop yacking! I'm wasting good money on this phone talking to you! In six German newspapers, published the day after I went to jail, there are photographs of Larry!'

'Why tell me? I know he's an Army deserter. I . . .'

'Can't you stop yacking and listen? He's not an Army deserter! He's an escapee from a Military prison where he was being held, waiting to be flown back to the States and to be put away for life in an asylum for the criminal insane!'

A wave of ice water seemed to run down Helga's spine.

'I – I don't believe it!'

'Why should I care? Don't believe it!' The voice was now a snarl of impatience. 'I'm telling you! The papers call him the Hamburg Strangler. He'd strangled five tarts before the cops caught up with him. He was tried and found guilty. It's all here in the papers. He escaped while waiting transport back to the States.'

She lay back on the pillow. Her heart was now beating sluggishly and she felt dreadfully cold.

'Oh, God!' she whispered.

'They say no one should go near him,' the voice went on. 'He's dangerous.'

She took hold of herself.

'But it was you who told him where to get the passport.'

'Sure . . . he seemed a nice kid to me. I've only just read this goddamn thing! When he phoned me and told me about this blackmail stunt I used my influence to help you . . . and I don't want your goddamn thanks. But when I read this in the papers, although I think you're worse than nothing, I had to warn you.'

Helga shivered.

'I'm alone here . . . he's in the next room!'

'Here's what you do. Lock yourself in . . . call the police and hope they get to you fast. So long, Mrs. Rolfe. I'm not sorry for you. Rich women with hot pants bore me and if Larry wrings your neck I won't cry. Call the police!'

The line went dead.

With a shaking hand, Helga replaced the receiver.

CHAPTER EIGHT

The Hamburg Strangler!

Helga's mind flashed back to three uneasy nights she had spent in New York when another strangler had been at large: a young man with a beguiling appearance who had picked up rich, lonely women in hotel lobbies, had persuaded them to take him to their rooms and who had left them strangled and mutilated. She remembered reading the horrifying details in the tabloid press. She had been there on business and had been yearning for a man, but when she had read the news that this killer was at large, she had become so nervous she had shunned every man who looked at her.

And now this!

She lay still.

A homicidal killer in her home!

Then she realized there was a complete silence in the villa. For a moment she couldn't understand why, then she realized that Larry had turned off the television set!

Her heart hammering painfully, she looked towards the door. The key was in the lock. Terror held her in a paralysing grip. She must lock the door! her mind screamed at her. She must call the police! But she found she was incapable of moving. She lay in the bed, cold, shaking and her breath coming in quick, short gasps.

Then she heard slow footfalls, muffled by the carpet in the corridor, but unmistakable.

She had told him to come to her room!

She stared at the key in the door and yet she still couldn't move. He was probably one of those awful sex maniacs who killed only when his lust was satisfied! She would be raped and then strangled!

She saw the door handle turn and she knew she had left it

too late. A scream inside her began to build up but died as the door opened.

Larry stood in the doorway. She stared up at him from her bed in horror. Terror misted her eyes. She could only make out his menacing bulk: his face was out of focus.

'Ma'am . . . don't be frightened of me. Please, ma'am. I can explain. Please listen to me.'

She made the effort and fought down her terror. His face swam into focus. Fear, misery and despair made him look helplessly immature and childishly harmless.

She lay there, staring at him, unable to form any words.

'When the phone went,' he said, 'I picked up the receiver. I did it automatically, ma'am. I wasn't spying. I heard what Ron said. It's all lies. I swear everything he told you are lies! Please believe me.'

'Go away,' Helga said huskily. 'Go away.'

Instead, he moved into the room, keeping away from the bed and he went over to an armchair by the window and sat in it. Then he put his hands to his face and began to cry. His soft blubbering lessened her terror. She wondered if she could get to the door, take out the key, get out and lock him in, but she decided that wouldn't be possible. She knew how quickly he could move.

'Stop it!' She tried to harden her voice. 'Please leave my room!'

'I don't know what I'll do if you won't believe me, ma'am,' he mumbled. 'You've been so kind to me. I'm so unhappy. You don't know how unhappy I am!'

The Hamburg Strangler! she thought. Five prostitutes! Yet, seeing him crouched in the chair, his hands covering his face, he looked so defenceless she began to gain confidence. He had said he was grateful to her, she reminded herself. Why should he harm her if she didn't show fear or irritate him. She would have to be very careful how she behaved to him and she must somehow get him out of the room so she could lock the door.

'I didn't know you were so unhappy, Larry,' she said gently. 'Will you tell me why?'

He took his hands from his face. Tears had made his face puffy and his misery touched her.

'I've been snowing you, ma'am ... all this time. After what you've done for me, I wanted to keep your respect.' He hesitated, then lowered his head so he didn't look at her. 'You'd better know the truth now ... I don't go for girls ...' He paused and mumbled something that Helga couldn't hear. 'What did you say?'

He gripped his knees with his huge hands.

'Larry ... what did you say?'

'I go for men.'

Helga regarded him unbelievingly.

'For men?'

He nodded miserably, not looking at her.

'But you said a girl took your money,' she said after a long pause. 'Archer told me when he first met you you were trying to pick up a tart.'

He looked up then and she saw the shame and misery in his eyes.

'It wasn't a girl who took my money ... it was a man.' He spoke so quietly she could scarcely hear him. 'That other girl ... I was trying to get her boy friend from her.'

Helga suddenly understood. This was, of course the answer to his indifference to her. In a perverse way what he was telling her pleased her. It meant that she hadn't lost her sex appeal, but she instantly dismissed this trivial thought. It would also explain why he had murdered five prostitutes. Certain homosexuals loathed prostitutes.

'You see, ma'am, Ron and I were close.' Larry looked away from her. 'He's like me. He wanted me and I wanted him, but I guess I'm restless. I don't like anything permanent ... I don't want to be tied down. A week with Ron was enough. I did desert from the Army, but what he told you were spiteful lies. I've never killed anyone.' He thumped his knees with his big fists. 'I guess I'm stupid. When you said you would pay my fare to New York and give me five thousand bucks, I just had to tell Ron. He had sworn I would come crawling back to Hamburg because I wouldn't be able to live without him. I wanted him to know I wasn't coming back and why. I told him how kind you had been to me and I was going back to the States and about the money.' He wiped his eyes with the back of his hand. 'That was stupid of me, ma'am. Ron flipped his lid. You see, ma'am, he just hated the idea you were helping me and he couldn't. He got in this terrible rage and he called me names. He was yelling and swearing at me. He said he would fix me. I couldn't stand listening to what he said so I hung up on him.'

'When did you call him?' Helga asked.

'When you went to the village. I just had to tell him . . . I was stupid.' He stared miserably at her. 'But I didn't think he would do anything. He often got wild, but he never did anything. I never thought he would call you and tell you all those lies. I heard him tell you to call the cops. That's what he wants. If they come here, they'll find out I'm AWOL. Ron knows if they pick me up, I'll be sent back to Hamburg and after I come out of the Stockade, he will be waiting for me. The fact is, ma'am, Ron likes me more than I like him. He can't live without me . . . I know he can't. That stuff about me being in the papers was all jealous lies . . . lies to make you call the cops.'

Helga drew in a long, deep breath. She had had many dealings with homosexuals. Her hairdresser in Paradise City was one. The Captain of Waiters at her favourite New York nightclub was another. Her Couturier in Paris and the simpering little artist who had decorated this bedroom . . . dozens of them in every walk of life who she loathed and despised and who she knew could be viciously jealous, envious and unpredictably spiteful to each other and yet, at times, so marvellously gentle and kind.

Yes, she could believe this story. She relaxed back on her pillow. God! How terrified she had been! The Hamburg Strangler! How stupid to have believed such a malicious story, let alone allow it to have frightened her so!

'You do believe me, ma'am? You won't call the police?'

So he was one of those! It was hard to believe as she looked at him, but where had she heard some all-in wrestler, wearing a cloak and a top hat, had been a pansy?

She suddenly hated the sight of this big, hulking boy. She wanted to scream at him to leave the villa this very moment, but then she remembered those awful moments when Archer had escaped. Larry had to remain here to control Archer until the photos arrived. With a sinking heart, she thought of the long day and the long night ahead of her before the photos did arrive.

'Yes, Larry, I believe you,' she said. 'I didn't understand ... I do now.'

'You don't know what hell it is in the Army when you're like me,' he said, half to himself. 'I couldn't stand any more of it.'

She didn't want to hear: he was a neuter thing to her now and he bored her.   'All right, Larry ... now go to bed.'

He got reluctantly to his feet.

'I'm sorry, ma'am. I didn't want you to know. You've been so good to me.'

'Yes ... go to bed!' She could scarcely conceal her impatience to be rid of him.

'Yes, ma'am.'

He walked to the door, hesitated, looked hopefully at her, then went out, closing the door gently behind him.

She lay still listening to his receding footfalls, then she put her hands to her face and began silently to laugh.

What a joke against her!

She had picked up this lump of maleness, longing to take him into her bed. She had spent money on him, fed him, dangled her charms before him, risked her reputation, risked sixty million dollars, had been blackmailed because of him and had had to listen to glib lies from another of his beastly breed who had terrified her as she had never been so terrified ... and for what? For trying to inveigle a loutish, immature, brainless queer into her bed!

What a goddamn joke!

Finally, her bitter laughter ceased. She got out of bed and locked the door. Going into the bathroom, she swallowed three sleeping tablets, then she got back into bed.

She thought of Nassau and its miles of golden beach.

There would be lots of men there ... real men. She would have to be careful, of course, but during the day, Herman would be fully occupied.

There would be opportunities ... there were always opportunities.

She reached up and turned off the light. She lay still in the darkness, willing herself not to think while she waited for the tablets to send her to sleep.

It wasn't until 10.25 the following morning when Helga emerged from her bedroom. She had slept heavily, but dreamlessly. She had a slight headache and she was in an irritable mood.

While she had bathed and dressed, she had thought of Larry and the desire grew in her to get rid of him as quickly as was safe.

'Coffee, ma'am?'

Larry was standing in the kitchen door. His expression was downcast and he avoided meeting her eyes.

'Thank you: that would be nice,' she said briskly and impersonally as if talking to a servant. She went to the front door and checked the mail box. There were several letters and she returned to the sitting-room, flicking through them. There were two letters for her from women friends back home and the rest were for Herman.

She was reading her letters when Larry brought in a tray with toast, marmalade and coffee.

'Nothing to eat,' she said without pausing in her reading. 'Thank you. Just put it down.'

He hung around like a child in disgrace, for some moments watching her reading, then as she paid no attention to him, he returned to the kitchen. She drank her coffee, completed reading the letters which were full of the latest 'Who-is-now-sleeping-with-whom' scandals and other gossipy items. After she had readdressed her husband's letters to Nassau, she went into the kitchen.

Larry was sitting on a kitchen chair, his big fists resting on his knees while he stared at the floor.

'I'm going now to the American Express to get your ticket,' she said. 'Also to the bank to get your money. I have other things to do in Lugano. I may be late back.'

She had no intention of spending the day with him. The time would go much faster watching a movie.

He looked up.

'Okay, ma'am.'

'How is he this morning?'

163

He rubbed the side of his jaw.

'He's okay.'

She was now utterly sick of Archer and utterly sick of Larry. 'Don't answer the telephone nor the front door.'

'No ma'am.'

She went into the hall and put on her coat. As she was struggling into her snow boots, he came to the kitchen door.

'You – you won't tell the cops, ma'am?'

She looked around impatiently.

'Oh step fretting! You will be flying to New York tomorrow afternoon.'

'Thank you, ma'am.'

'You have plenty of food. I may have dinner out . . . if I do I won't be back until ten-thirty tonight. You have the television to amuse you.' She opened the front door. 'And don't do anything stupid down there . . . like last time.'

'No, ma'am.' His hangdog expression bored her.

'Just be careful.'

She went down the steps into the cold sunshine.

What a relief to get out of the villa and away from this poor creature, she thought as she opened the garage doors. One more night and the nightmare would be over. She backed the car out of the garage and drove down to the main road.

She had trouble finding parking in Lugano, but eventually, after circling patiently for twenty minutes, she saw a car pull out from a parking meter. By fast driving, she managed to foil an Alfa whose driver had also been circling for some time. He scowled at her as he drove on. She put a twenty centime piece into the meter, then walked to the American Express office. There, she booked a Tourist class ticket for Larry on the following day at 14.00 and for herself first class on the same day but at 22.05 for New York. She had no intention of flying to New York with Larry. She would drive him to Milan airport and make sure he left, then she would leave the car with a garage with instructions it was to be returned to Castagnola and left in the garage at the villa. She would spend the time until the flight at the *Principe e savoia* hotel where she was known and where she would be pampered.

She used her American Express Credit card to take care of the two fares, then she walked across the Reforma Square to the *Credit Suisse Banque*. Here, she asked for $5,000 in unsigned Travellers' Cheques. While she was waiting, the manager of the bank came from his office to shake hands with her and to inquire after her husband. This kindness and deference she was receiving from the bank manager pleased and flattered her, but she wondered, a little cynically, if, without money, she would have received the same treatment.

She then walked through the old shopping centre, shop window gazing. She wasn't in the mood to buy, but the goods displayed interested her and helped to pass the time.

She returned to the Mercedes and drove along the lake side to the Eden hotel. Leaving the car in the hotel garage, she went to the Grill room. A table was quickly found for her and the *Maître d'hotel* came to shake hands. She broke the news to him that Herman would not be coming to Lugano this year and his face fell. She ordered devilled scampi with wild rice and lingered over the meal, being in no hurry. After coffee and paying her check, she walked slowly along the lake side to the Casino cinema. They were showing Katie Hepburn in *The Lion In Winter*. She adored this actress and she felt an anticipation of excitement as she bought her ticket. She sat in the darkness and the warmth of the cinema and concentrated on the film. Hepburn didn't disappoint her: a wonderful, professional performance, she thought as she came out into the cold. She wandered back in the gathering gloom to the Eden hotel, analysing and remembering certain scenes of the film and re-enjoying it.

Not once since she had left the villa did she think of Larry or Archer. She settled in the comfortable hotel bar with a copy of the *Herald Tribune* and a vodka martini. Having spent some time checking the Stock Market quotations, she read the news, had another cocktail and then decided it was time for dinner.

Leaving the hotel, she drove back to the Reforma and was lucky to find a free parking meter. Then she walked to her favourite restaurant, *Bianchi* in via Pessina. Here she was given a warm welcome by Dino, one of the head waiters and who always looked after her. He was a good looking Italian with beautiful manners. As he conducted her to a table, he inquired after Mr. Rolfe and sighed when he learned he wasn't coming this year.

Seated, she asked him what she should eat. The partridges were very good, he told her, but she shook her head. Then venison. A little Puccini toast and a coeur de chevreuil. She agreed and he went away to place the order.

It was early and the restaurant hadn't begun to get busy so Dino returned to gossip. Then the Patron came over to have a word. Helga relaxed in this friendly, cosseted atmosphere. The Puccini toast was served and an excellent Merlot wine poured.

She enjoyed the impeccable meal and finished regretfully at 21.40. She paid the check, shook hands with the Patron, had a word with Dino and returned to her car. It was only when she was starting the engine that she began to think of Larry.

Immediately, she began to feel a little uneasy. Perhaps she shouldn't have left him so long. He was such a hick he might have done something stupid. She herself would look stupid if on her return she found Archer waiting for her and Larry imprisoned in the cellar. But she had warned Larry. Surely he must have learned his lesson? She couldn't possibly have spent all those hours alone with him. The very sight of him now sickened her.

Driving towards Castagnola, her uneasiness increased. Suppose Archer had got out? By now the photos would be in the post. If he had trapped Larry and was free, he would wait, guarding the cellar door until the postman arrived. The envelope would be addressed to him. Then she thought of the .22 automatic she had in her bedroom. She had everything to lose. She wouldn't hesitate to shoot him in the leg if he refused when threatened by the gun to return to the cellar and to release Larry. She felt sure he wouldn't have the guts to oppose her after she had fired one shot towards him, threatening the next shot would be in his leg.

The Grandfather clock in the hall was chiming eleven as she unlocked the front door. She stood in the open doorway, her heart skipping a beat. *The pole that had jammed the*

*cellar door was lying on the floor and the cellar door stood
open!*

What was happening?

She moved into the hall and closed the front door. Was
Larry downstairs with Archer? Perhaps he had gone down
there with food, but surely that was unlikely at this hour.

'She went silently to the head of the stairs leading down to
the cellars and listened, but she could hear nothing. The
light in the passage below was on.

She hesitated, then called, 'Larry? Are you down there?'

A sound behind her made her spin around.

Archer was standing in the sitting-room doorway, a
whisky and soda in his hand. The bruise on his face had
deepened to an ugly purple-black.

'Larry's in here, Helga,' he said. 'Take off your coat and
come on in. We've been waiting for you. Did you have a
pleasant day?'

She kept control of herself as she took off her coat and hat.
She paused to fluff up her hair with fingers that trembled.

Archer turned and went back into the room, leaving the
door open.

Helga felt fury grip her: fury against herself. Her disgust,
contempt and frustration had made staying with this hulking queer impossible. She should have controlled those feelings. Now she was going to pay for them.

She entered the sitting-room. Archer was standing by a
lounging chair, waiting for her. Across the room, Larry was
sitting on an upright chair, his hands hanging between his
knees, his head down so she couldn't see his face.

'Sit down, Helga,' Archer said.

She was glad to sit down. Once again her legs felt weak
and once again she was struggling to absorb a shock.

'Excuse me.' He walked up to her and took her handbag
from her before she realized what he was doing.

'How dare you!' she exclaimed but without conviction.

'Come off your high horse, Helga. You're not in a position
to get snooty.' Archer backed away, opened the bag and took
from it one of the air tickets and the leather folder containing the Travellers' Cheques. He carried them across the
room and put them on an occasional table by Larry.

'There you are, my boy,' he said. 'Your ticket and your money . . . now you get off.'

Helga watched.

Larry didn't look up. He just sat slumped in his chair, his head down.

'Come along, Larry,' Archer said in his soothing, professional voice. 'There's no point in you hanging around here any longer. Take Helga's car and leave it at the Lugano station. I'm sure she won't mind and she can pick it up later. There's a train to Milan you could catch if you hurry.'

Slowly, Larry got to his feet. He picked up the ticket and the leather folder and stuffed them into his hip pocket. Then he looked directly at Archer.

'I don't want her car . . . I don't want anything from you.'

His voice was a mumble and Helga could scarcely make out what he was saying.

'All right, Larry . . . you handle it,' Archer said. 'Good luck . . . have a good trip.'

Walking heavily, Larry made for the door. As he opened the door, Helga said huskily, 'Haven't you anything to say to me?'

He didn't appear to hear her. He went out and through the open door. She watched him open the front door and go out into the darkness. The front door shut behind him.

She closed her eyes.

There was a long pause, then Archer said, 'Well, he's gone. I'm sure you are puzzled, Helga. He lowered his bulk into an armchair. Taking his cigar case from his pocket, he selected a cigar and bit off the end. 'Let me explain. Up to this morning, I have always regarded you as a clever and astute woman. You have disappointed me. To be successful in dealing with people, one needs to have a certain amount of psychological insight. This I thought you had. but obviously you haven't. You were so besotted by Larry's bulk and his apparent virility that you failed to realize he was a homo. That was a mistake and a bad one. I spotted it, not immediately, but soon enough to understand that he would need different handling from the way you were handling him. The one thing a homo dislikes more than anything else is contempt. He will put up with the jokes and giggles: these are things he has come to live with, but he hates contempt. So long as you thought you could drag him into your bed, you gave him kindness which he was thirsting for: all homos do. In actual fact, Helga, Larry is rather a nice boy. He's stupid, of course, immature, doesn't know his own strength, but basically he is simple and nice and there is no real viciousness in him. He is handicapped by his size. He would be a lot happier if he had been a pretty boy, but as he looks like an athlete, he has tried to give people who don't spot what he really is a false image of himself drawn, no doubt, from the toughs he has seen on television. The scowl and the hard voice are marks to encourage those who think he is just another hard guy in a leather jacket and jeans. All rather pathetic really because his own breed recognize him instantly.' Archer paused to light his cigar. 'You couldn't have played a better card for me and a worse card for yourself when you reacted the way you did after Larry had told you the truth about himself. I realize you were frustrated and bitter that you weren't going to drag him into your bed, but where was your psychological insight? Instead of being understanding and sympathetic, you were stupid enough to show him your true feelings: disgust and contempt. From the moment you knew, you treated him like something unclean ... like a leper, you might say, and you hurt him, Helga. You hurt him deeply, and you are so insensitive you didn't even care that you had hurt him. He admired and respected you and even loved you in an odd way because up to the moment he told you what he was, you had overwhelmed him with kindness. This morning, you behaved even more stupidly if you were hoping to keep him as an ally. Without saying it in so many words, you told him you couldn't bear to stay a minute longer in his company and your contempt was like a branding iron on his very sensitive skin. You walked out on him. I was at the cellar door, listening. The contempt in your voice when you told him to amuse himself with television and you wouldn't be back until late, leaving him alone, told me, because of your complete lack of understanding that you had once again handed me the four aces.'

Helga listened. Her mind was beginning to function again. Larry was gone. Now only Archer and she were left in the villa. Tomorrow morning the photos would arrive. She thought of the gun. It was she who held the four aces. With the gun, she would get and destroy the photos even if she had to shoot this thief, forger and blackmailer.

She looked at Archer, her face expressionless.

'Yes, I was stupid,' she said and lifted her shoulders. 'Well, one has to pay for being stupid.'

He regarded her watchfully.

'You are a fantastic woman, Helga.' There was a note of admiration in his voice. 'Your dangerous, sharp brain is already working to find a way out, but I assure you, this time, there is no way out. We are back to square A.'

'Are we?' Again she lifted her shoulders. 'But tell me more about Larry. How did you and he get buddies? I know you are supposed to be able to charm a bird off a tree, but I never imagined you could charm a pansy to confide in you.'

Archer blew cigar smoke towards the ceiling.

'Have a brandy?' He picked up his glass and stood up. Helga noted that he walked a little unsteadily. He had probably been drinking most of the evening while waiting for her and her eyes narrowed.

'No, thank you.'

He went to the bar and refilled his glass.

'I consider myself an amateur psychologist. When you had gone I went back to the the games room and I prepared for a long wait. I heard Larry roaming around the villa: ceaselessly pacing up and down and I knew he was suffering. He didn't know what to do with himself. Obviously, he was very lonely. Around two o'clock, he came down with my lunch. I was lying on the settee, waiting for him, knowing this was my chance. I made out I was much more feeble than I was to lull his alertness. After all, he had beaten me up, so I moaned a little. I could see he was unhappy and uneasy. He had cooked me a couple of lamb chops; they looked most tempting. I said I would try to eat them and I thanked him as only I know how to thank people for taking so much trouble. He was thirsting for kindness.' Archer gave a snorting laugh. 'It was rather pathetic to see his confusion at being so praised. I asked where you were and he told me you had gone out for the day. I saw his expression of resentment and how hurt he was. I said it couldn't be much fun for him to be on his own in this big villa and should we talk while I ate my lunch? It was easy after that, Helga. I talked about you, I told him that you had married an enormously wealthy cripple for his money and how you've never stopped cheating him. I told him about the men you have had. Perhaps I exaggerated a little, but it was necessary to get him on my side. He remembered how you had fumbled at his zipper and that had shocked him: it didn't go along with his image of you as a kind, blonde madonna. I said you were utterly immoral, that you used men to service your body and after, threw them aside. I told him your only interest in him was his body and when you found you weren't going to get that, you couldn't stand the sight of him. I reminded him you would be returning with his money and ticket to New York. I said you deserved to be punished and he could do it. "Take what she gives you and walk out on her ... leave her to me", I said. He liked the idea. He wanted you to suffer for the way you had treated him. So we waited together for you to return. Now he's gone, Helga, and you and I will finalize this little drama. It's time we did. I fly back to Lausanne at seven o'clock tomorrow morning.'

Helga looked up sharply.

'So early?'

The postman, she thought, didn't come to the villa until after ten.

'Yes. I have appointments I can't afford to miss. Well now, Helga, you have played your cards badly and I have played them well so accept defeat. You will tell Herman it was your idea and not mine to buy the Nickel shares and you will insist that I keep the account.'

'The postman doesn't come until after ten. When the photos arrive, we'll discuss this further. You'll have to cancel your appointments.'

He regarded her, then he began to shake with silent laughter. Watching his face turn red and his paunch jerking as he laughed, she felt cold despair grip her. She had a frightening feeling that in the grimly fought battle of lies and violence he had finally beaten her. He couldn't laugh like this unless he was very sure of himself.

'I take it the joke is on me?' she said, her voice hard.

He wiped his streaming eyes with his handkerchief, gasped, coughed and then slapped his fat knees.

'That's the understatement of the year,' he said. 'Learn a lesson, Helga . . . never try to bluff with me.' He leaned back in his chair and grinned at her: a smirking, triumphant grin that made her heart sink. 'In a few minutes, I am leaving for Lugano. I intend to spend a comfortable night at the Eden, then at seven tomorrow I will fly to Lausanne. *I* don't need to wait for the postman who *you* are so anxiously waiting for.' He became convulsed with laughter again, but this time it wasn't silent. His raucous ha! ha! ha's! were like the thong of a whip cutting her flesh.

She waited, now dangerous fury boiling up inside her. Her hands into fists, she watched him and a feeling grew in her to hurt or even kill him.

Finally, his laughter subsided and again he mopped his eyes. 'You poor fool!' His eyes were now cold and contemptuous. 'I never sent those photos to the bank! I was bluffing! They have been in my suitcase all the time!'

The blow was a savage one and it left her breathless. Her mind went back to those moments when she had stopped Larry from beating him up, when he had lied about his bad heart. She thought of Larry making the dangerous fast drive back to Basle, of the three thousand five hundred francs she had paid for the forged signature and of the long, tormenting hours believing that when the postman eventually came, she would be safe.

And all the time the photos had been in his suitcase, lying in the back of his hired car which she had seen, which had been there for the taking!

But now she knew the photos were within reach! He didn't know it yet, but she still held the four aces. She had the gun!

She got slowly to her feet, her handkerchief pressed to her lips.

'I – I think I'm going to be sick,' she whispered and started across the room, then as she reached the door, she moved faster. In the hall, she ran frantically to her bedroom, pulled open the closet door, wrenched open the top drawer and her hand closed over the .22 gun.

As she picked up the gun the savage feeling that had been growing in her to kill him again ran through her. If he didn't give her the photographs she would kill him! She didn't give a damn about the consequences! He had made her suffer as she had never thought it possible to suffer! He had sneered and laughed at her! It wouldn't be a shot in the leg ... she would kill him!

Her breath was coming through her open mouth in short, hard, rasping gasps. Her heart was slamming against her ribs. But this wouldn't do, she told herself. Shaking, gasping and half out of her mind as she was would make a deadly shot impossible.

'Helga?' Archer called. 'Are you all right?'

She drew in a long shuddering breath, then again. She steadied herself. Her heart ceased to race but still thumped painfully. Keeping the gun down by her side and out of sight, she walked back into the sitting-room.

Archer, sitting in the armchair, regarded her with an amused smile.

'Did you chuck up?' he asked. 'I didn't think you were quite so sensitive.'

'You will give me the photos,' she said in a husky whisper, 'or I'll kill you!' She lifted the gun into sight.

'How dramatic you are.' He got to his feet. 'I'm leaving now. Have a good time in Nassau. Watch out for the boys there, Helga. Don't let Herman catch you at it.' He bent to stub out his cigar. 'So it is understood? You take the blame for buying the shares and I keep the account?'

'I mean it? Give me the photographs! I don't give a damn what happens to me! Give them to me or I'll kill you!'

He gave a snorting laugh and walked towards the door.

'Attractive as you are, Helga there are times when you bore me,' he said as he opened the door.

She aimed the gun at his broad, fat back and with a shudder, she pulled the trigger. Only the snap of the hammer greeted her.

He looked around, lifting his eyebrows.

'I'm surprised at you, Helga. A whore ... now a murderess? So you would have done it. I wasn't sure so I took the precaution to find your little toy and unload it. Admit I'm smarter than you. Goodbye. Convince Herman and remember never to try to bluff with me again. I'm a lot better at it than you.'

She stood motionless, shivering, staring at the empty gun in her hand. She heard the front door slam, then she walked slowly to a chair and sank into it. She heard a car engine start up and the car drive away.

Then she began to weep. She had always thought she was smarter than Archer. She had always been slightly contemptuous of his abilities, but the sonofabitch had beaten her! He had out-bluffed her in every move and now she would have to have him on her neck until Herman died!

She beat on the back of her chair with her fists as she cried in frustration and bitter rage. A slob like that! Now she would have to face Herman and admit she hadn't been capable of handling his money: that she had been responsible for losing two million dollars!

'Ma'am?'

She started, stiffened and looked up.

Larry was standing in the doorway.

The shock of seeing him made her speechless. She could only stare at him, fighting back the tearing sobs that were racking her.

'It's all right, ma'am,' he said and moving into the room, he dropped a manilla envelope into her lap. 'You don't have to cry like that.'

With shaking hands, she tore open the flap of the envelope and pulled out two glossy prints: one of her handing money to Friedlander and the other of her naked on the bed with Larry. She peered into the envelope. The negatives were there.

'Better burn them right away, ma'am,' Larry said.

'How did you get them?'

'I knew he was up to something. I wanted you to have them. I pretended to go along with him but I came back and listened. I heard him tell you they were in his suitcase. I went to his car and found them.'

She picked up a cigarette lighter, flicked the flame into life and held it to the photographs. She dropped the ash into the ash tray, then she did the same with the negatives.

'I'm sorry,' she said brokenly, looking at him. 'I'm really sorry, Larry, for the way I've behaved.'

'That's okay, ma'am.' He put the air ticket and the Travellers' cheques in their leather folder on the table. 'You were good to me too. This makes us quits. I'm going back to Hamburg. So long, ma'am.'

She struggled to her feet and caught hold of his arm.

'Don't be stupid, Larry! Take this money and go back to the States! You must! Start a new life! I'll drive you to Milan. I'll give you more money! You don't know what you've done for me! I can never forget it!'

He pulled away from her as if her touch was unclean.

'No, thank you, ma'am. I don't want any more help from you.' He looked at her and she flinched from the accusing expression in his eyes. 'You and Archer are filth to me. I don't like saying this to you, but it's the truth. I didn't know people like you existed. I'm going back to the Army and I'll serve my sentence, then I'll be out in another year. I did this for you because of what you did for me, but I never want to see you again.'

'You mean you're going back to Ron?'

'Ron is better than you. Yes, I'm going back to him. He doesn't cheat and he's honest.'

Helga lifted her hands helplessly.

'All right. I hope you will be happy with him, Larry, and thank you again.'

He went to the door, paused, turned and pulled at the peak of his cap.

'So long, ma'am. I hope you'll be happy too.'

Her mind now was no longer with him. She was thinking of Archer. She would throw him to the wolves. Then Nassau, the sand, the sea and the sun. It would be good to lie in the sun and to think of Archer in the Establissement de l'Orbe in a small cell for at least five years.

She heard the front door shut. After a long pause, she went into the hall and turned the front door key.

CRIME TITLES AVAILABLE FROM CORGI BOOKS

WHILE EVERY EFFORT IS MADE TO KEEP PRICES LOW, IT IS SOME-
TIMES NECESSARY TO INCREASE PRICES AT SHORT NOTICE. CORGI
BOOKS RESERVE THE RIGHT TO SHOW AND CHARGE NEW RETAIL
PRICES ON COVERS WHICH MAY DIFFER FROM THOSE ADVERTISED
IN THE TEXT OR ELSEWHERE.

THE PRICES SHOWN BELOW WERE CORRECT AT THE TIME OF
GOING TO PRESS (JANUARY '86).

☐	10426 4	Joker in the Pack	*James Hadley Chase*	£1.50
☐	11558 4	Well Now My Pretty	*James Hadley Chase*	£1.50
☐	11356 5	The Way the Cookie Crumbles	*James Hadley Chase*	£1.50
☐	10522 8	No Orchids for Miss Blandish	*James Hadley Chase*	£1.50
☐	10574 0	Do Me a Favour, Drop Dead	*James Hadley Chase*	£1.50
☐	11646 7	Come Easy, Go Easy	*James Hadley Chase*	95p
☐	11506 1	Believed Violent	*James Hadley Chase*	£1.75
☐	09648 2	Have a Change of Scene	*James Hadley Chase*	£1.75
☐	10765 4	Mallory	*James Hadley Chase*	£1.75
☐	09424 2	An Ace Up My Sleeve	*James Hadley Chase*	£1.75
☐	10328 4	Lady, Here's Your Wreath	*James Hadley Chase*	£1.75
☐	11090 6	Goldilocks	*Ed McBain*	£1.50
☐	12021 9	Rumpelstiltskin	*Ed McBain*	£1.50
☐	12203 3	Beauty and the Beast	*Ed McBain*	£1.75

*All these books are available at your bookshop or newsagent, or can be ordered direct from the
publisher. Just tick the titles you want and fill in the form below.*

CORGI BOOKS, Cash Sales Department, P.O Box 11, Falmouth, Cornwall.

Please send cheque or postal order, no currency.

Please allow cost of book(s) plus the following for postage and packing:

U.K. CUSTOMERS – Allow 55p for the first book, 22p for the second book and 14p
for each additional book ordered, to a maximum charge of £1.75.

B.F.P.O. & EIRE – Allow 55p for the first book, 22p for the second book plus 14p
per copy for the next seven books, thereafter 8p per book.

OVERSEAS CUSTOMERS – Allow £1.00 for the first book and 25p per copy for
each additional book.

NAME (Block Letters) ....

ADDRESS ....

....